SIN SHIP

SIN SHIP

J.T. PRITCHARD

CUTTING EDGE

ISBN-13: 978-1-957868-77-6

Published by
Cutting Edge Books
PO Box 8212
Calabasas, CA 91372
www.cuttingedgebooks.com

TABLE OF CONTENTS

CHAPTER ONE
UNAPPROACHABLE VENUS

THE pounding at the cabin door grew louder, more drunkenly insistent.

"No," the girl whispered to herself. Please, please no ... Don't let him touch me again! Don't let him ... "

Blue eyes widened in terror, she watched the knob turn furiously back and forth. Backing until she had flattened herself against the opposite wall, she let her fingers crawl nervous patterns along the smooth, waxed paneling. Her honey-colored hair, softly lovely even in disorder, fell over her bare and trembling shoulders, half concealing the gaping rent where the sheer, green shantung had been roughly ripped open. A full-length mirror was set into the light door which stood between her and the sickening thing outside, and she had a sudden, hysterical sense of watching herself as in a nightmare.

It couldn't be happening. In a moment she would wake up, snug in her tiny apartment with the collection of glass animals on the mantlepiece, the philodendron plant lightly named Oscar, her name, Betty Brooks, under the doorbell —

But it *was* real! The yacht was real, the oak paneling of the cabin was solid under her moist palms. The warm flush of her body, brought on by fright and one too many extra-strong cocktails — this was real. And the thick, excited voice that called to her through the locked door — that was hideously, starkly real. It was the voice of Bobby Morgan.

Yes, *that* Bobby Morgan. The one whose escapades had been making copy for every yellow tabloid in the country, ever since he had been expelled from the first of half a dozen colleges, fifteen years ago. Bobby Morgan, the playboy who used the world for his back yard, tossing away a fortune every year — but somehow never managing to spend his money faster than his family's vast enterprises accumulated it. Bobby Morgan, whose name had been linked with scandals so unsavory that even the most sycophantic columnists had been obliged to give up their usual boys-will-be-boys attitude and chide him gently.

"Betty!" he called. "Stop being a little fool, and open that door. I don't go for this hard-to-get act — "

Betty found her voice and spoke back to cut short the sickening, callous insinuation. Just what did the fellow think she was?

"Before I'd even look at you again," she said, "I'd — I'd kill myself!"

Bobby's laugh was sardonic, threaded with a subtle cruelty.

"I hardly think so," he replied. "You're too healthy a specimen to try that. Only sick people make that mistake, and I find you wonderfully, refreshingly healthy. So I'll simply sit down here and wait for you to come to your senses. Of course, I'm not the most patient man in the world, so if you refuse to be realistic — well, please remember that this is *my* yacht. In my own cabin I keep a duplicate set of keys for every lock on her. I hope I won't have to use them. But think it over."

Betty heard his shoulders settle against the door as he made himself comfortable. She shuddered. Her even white teeth nibbled her full lower lip as her glance darted about the cabin. There must be something — *something* she could do...

Real *class.* That was how Rocky, her boss at the Deep Sea Club, referred to Bobby Morgan and his gang. Rocky's idea of a gentleman was someone who could afford to come into his gin mill night after night, lose consistently at the crooked wheels in the gambling rooms upstairs, and keep coming back, season after season, without complaint. His idea of a lady was somewhat more vague, perhaps because he felt that he had yet to meet one. But Rocky recognized an opportunity when he saw one, and one night he stopped at the checkroom where Betty worked. He waited until she had given a customer his hat, watched to be sure that she dropped the tip into the slotted box, and then lit into her.

Oh not loudly, or in such a manner as to attract attention — that wasn't Rocky's way. He smiled, and his voice was soft. But the smile was cold, and under the quiet of his voice a razor-sharp edge flickered.

"You like your job here?" he asked.

She didn't. She hated it. Hated the cheapness and the false mask of gaiety over the tawdry lives that were wasted in places like the club. She hated the spying, the thugs Rocky sent in posing as customers, with orders to overtip the cigaret girls, the camera girls and herself with marked bills — because the tips were Rocky's, except for a small percentage which he figured out himself. She hated the noisy, thin-lipped racketeers and their brassy, over-dressed women. She hated the jaded crowd of wastrels, drifting without purpose in a world of too much money and too little character. And she hated the things she had seen — girls in their teens, at a time when their awakening womanhood sang within them, stumbling out on the arm of some smirking roué, their senses stunned by a calculated overdose of alcohol so that their fresh, young bodies might the more easily be possessed and despoiled in furtive, unlovely moments in some dark and lonely lane.

Rocky smiled humorlessly as she hesitated.

"Maybe I should say, do you *need* your job here," he said.

But he already knew the answer to that — had shrewdly guessed it on the day she had been hired. He really didn't need another checkroom girl, but if he could save a few dollars ... He had offered her ten dollars less than he was then paying, and Betty had accepted it, not knowing until days later that her acceptance had cost another girl her job.

"I hear you been smart with some of the customers," he went on. "Like some of Bobby Morgan's crowd. They like to kid, and you act like the Queen of Sheba or something. Like maybe you don't care to mingle with small fry."

He blew a fat ring of cigar smoke reflectively toward the ceiling.

"Maybe I made a mistake, hiring a college graduate for this job. Maybe the Randolphs and the Woodwards and the Morgans ain't good enough for you."

"That's — that's ridiculous," Betty exclaimed. "I've been perfectly courteous to Mr. Morgan, even if I don't like him. Once or twice, it's true, he's tried to — well, to date me, and I've had to refuse, but —"

"Why," Rocky's voice crackled, "Why did you have to refuse?"

Betty sought for words to express her feelings in a way that Rocky could understand.

"Well, I just don't like him," she said finally. "Tonight, when he asked me to join a party out on his yacht...You know what those parties of his are like, what it means to get mixed up in a thing like that."

"I don't know nothin'," Rocky answered. "I'm not a college graduate like you. But I know how to run this business, and I know better than to keep somebody who chases the customers away. I know that I could get half a dozen good-looking chicks to take your job in a minute. I know that most girls would give their eyeteeth to get in with Morgan's crowd. And I know that any smart girl doesn't have to give away anything she doesn't want to. And I think you know it too, even if I never tried to find out."

He paused to let this sink in, and then continued.

"It means a lot to me to keep Bobby's crowd coming back. Enough so I wouldn't mind giving a girl a week off to go on one of his cruises, like the one I hear he's planning for the next few days. And it isn't like I was asking her to go off alone with him — I'm not in *that* business, and there's always a big bunch along when Bobby's on a binge. She'd meet people — important people, real class — have the time of her life ... "

He dropped the sodden cigar into an ashtray for Betty to dispose of.

"I've got a little bet on you, kid," he concluded. "Figuring how tough things are right now, I'm betting that if Bobby Morgan asks you out again, you'll be smart. I'm so sure of it that I'm betting your job on it."

And with that he walked away. It was two nights later when Betty was forced to make a decision.

She had hoped that somehow Bobby would ignore her, that his unstable enthusiasm would be attracted elsewhere. But, followed into the place by his usual retinue of hangers-on, Bobby whooped with delight when he saw her.

"The unattainable Betty!" He greeted her. "Unapproachable Aphrodite, garrisoned about by the strength of her own virtue! Guardian alike of my fedora and her womanly honor, she willingly surrenders one on receipt of a brass check. The other, I fear, she reserves for a gold finger-band."

The people with him laughed. Bobby looked hurt, his dissolutely handsome face wrinkling in mock chagrin.

"No smile?" he asked. "No sign of welcome to bid us free to spend our shekels in this emporium of a thousand delights, this glorified penny-arcade of fugitive excitements? Fie, girl, fie!"

"Bobby, you're impossible," giggled a woman who rubbed her shoulder familiarly against the lapel of his dinner jacket.

Out of the corner of her eye Betty saw Rocky watching her. Across her mind flashed the long weeks of trudging from agency to agency before she had found work here. She remembered the tiny bank account which melted away as though by magic, the breakfastless mornings, the wakeful, anxious nights. And more — she remembered the mountain of business debts which comprised the only legacy her father had left — debts which she had resolved to pay in full, to keep faith with the man who had been both mother and father to her since her mother's death in bearing her.

She forced a smile.

She felt soiled, as though she had sold something of herself, but she smiled. Rocky turned away and lighted another cigar.

Late that night, as Bobby was leaving, he stopped at the checkroom and let the others go out ahead of him. Strangely enough, he appeared to be completely sober, and his previous boisterous manner had changed to one of subdued geniality.

"I'm a persistent cuss, Betty," he said when they were alone. "I've already been turned down twice when I asked you to drop in on one of my parties, but I just don't seem to learn. So I'll try again. I'm taking *The Dolphin* out for a week's run, sailing tomorrow at midnight. The destination — well, that's to be a surprise for everybody. I'd like you to come, if you feel that you can — we're not such an impossible bunch of boors when you get to know us."

"I . . I don't know," Betty hedged. "I'm a working girl, you know. I can't just drop everything whenever I feel a sudden urge to go on a cruise."

"Then if that's your only objection, I'm sure I can count you as one of my guests. I've already put out a few feelers in Rocky's direction, because it wouldn't have been fair to ask you, if you were going to be unable to leave the salt mines for a few days. But Rocky tells me you're due for some time off. So the answer is yes?"

A voice within whispered a warning, but Betty closed her mind to it. After all, she told herself, she was twenty-two years old and perfectly capable of taking care of herself.

"I suppose it is," she said with a nervous laugh. "You seem to have covered the objections pretty well."

"Good," Bobby said, waving his hat at someone who had come back to look for him. "I'll stop for you at three tomorrow.

Don't disappoint me now." He went out protestingly on the arm of his friend, trying to write down her address as he was led laughingly away.

Rocky patted her paternally on the shoulder when she told him of Bobby's invitation. She crawled inwardly, even though she knew he meant nothing by it. Some rival gangsters, she had heard, had beaten him up several years ago, and they had done something to him which left him unable to live a normal life where women were concerned.

"Now you're being smart, kid," he told her. "Go ahead and take the week off. We'll call it a vacation with pay, huh? Only listen, keep your ears open. Anything you hear — well, remember, Rocky will be glad to hear it too."

So she had gone, and now — now she heard Bobby stirring restlessly in the passageway. She was caught. Trapped, like a frantic mouse with which the cat toys. There was no one to turn to for help, for in Bobby's crowd like had found like, and under the thin veneer of sophistication and cleverness lay a cynical heartlessness. Anyone to whom she turned would simply laugh. They were, she told herself, like a decadent circus crowd of dying Rome's last days, demanding ever greater thrills, scornful of human values and moral law.

The slap of the sea against the sides of the anchored yacht suggested a possible escape. But no — the porthole was too small for her to crawl through. She gazed out of it toward the twinkling lights which sprinkled the beach. She could almost make out the neon-glow of the Deep Sea Club. If she could only get off the yacht! It wasn't too far to shore, and she was an excellent swimmer. But there wasn't a chance.

Sinking to a luxurious hassock, she faced the door and fought back the tears which brimmed up. She was waiting, staring fascinatedly at her own reflection. Waiting... for what? Something — *something* — must happen. The tide was running strong by now, and within an hour they would weigh anchor. Once they were under way her situation would be hopeless. The crew was well paid to notice nothing.

They were to sail at midnight, she knew. Where? Bobby and his captain knew where. For her, a voyage to hell.

CHAPTER TWO

PUSS IN THE CORNER

S HE had felt misgivings about Bobby's invitation from the beginning, and several times before she was actually on board she had been within a hair's breadth of turning back, of making some excuse. Finally she packed a small bag, and was pacing her room in a fury of indecision when Bobby and some of his friends called for her in mid-afternoon. They had been drinking — she had expected that — but everything seemed quite normal as she stepped into Bobby's yellow convertible — a huge, deep-voiced monster aglitter with chrome and equipped with a hundred unexpected accessories — and settled herself in the wide, leopard-skin seat.

Oh, perhaps some of the remarks had been a bit off-color, one or two jokes not in the best taste; still, there was nothing to indicate the inate viciousness she was to encounter. The little caravan of three cars rolled lazily down to the yacht basin, where a power launch waited to taxi them out to Bobby's craft.

The luxury of the yacht was breathtaking. No expense had been spared to make it a tiny floating palace. During the war, Betty was told, the boat had been stripped to bare essentials and had seen service with the Navy, but no trace of that grim austerity was now evident. A designer with a free hand had conceived a dream, and Bobby's wealth had brought the dream to actuality. Still, even as she marveled, Betty was not able to forget that half a dozen families could have lived for years just on what it cost to keep that expensive toy for one month.

There were already several people on board when Betty made her way up the side, and throughout the afternoon others arrived at sporadic intervals, so that it seemed she was continually being introduced to someone she had not seen before. A crew member showed her to the cabin which was to be hers, and there Betty changed into a tailored, lime-colored play-suit before returning to the deck. Bobby had whistled softly when she appeared, had set down his glass to take her by the shoulders and turn her slowly around for an appraising scrutiny.

"Well!" he exclaimed. "I always did wonder just what was under that evening gown you wear at the club. And now that I know part of the story, I must say that I'm not disappointed."

He stared frankly at her long, lithe thighs, rounded like carefully turned wood, lightly toasted by afternoons on the beach, the sun-bleached sprinkle of delicate hair little more than a hint of the softest peach-fuzz. Below her knees her calves swelled gently, tapering smoothly to her slender ankles, and Bobby's eyes missed not one subtle line, down to her very toes, peeping pinkly from her openwork huaraches. But Betty sensed that in his mind's eye this was not all that Bobby Morgan saw.

She sensed it, and felt strangely naked, as though his glance had somehow stripped her. More than that — she felt that others about them sensed it also, that they saw her, briefly, with Bobby's eyes. There was a moment of odd silence as the playboy's experienced inspection flicked over her loveliness like a light whiplash. In that instant the thought came to Betty that so might have stood some bartered girl of the ancient East, to be ogled and gloated over in the burning sunlight of the slave-block...

"For heaven's sake, Bobby," a voice broke in, "aren't you going to offer the girl a drink?"

Betty turned and caught the direct, knowing look of the girl who spoke, the cynical half-smile on the bright slash of mouth.

"By all means," laughed Bobby, reaching for a cocktail shaker. "In fact, I intend to see to it that she has several drinks."

Little by little, as the afternoon waned, the party began to grow less inhibited. Here and there couples paired off to make love — or what passed for love — with an alcoholic indifference to any audience. Occasionally a couple disappeared on some pretext or other which scarcely served to veil their real purpose. But for the most part, Betty intuitively understood, they were waiting for night to fall, for darkness to cover raw passions which could not meet the honest light of day.

She considered going for a swim — a large rubber raft had been inflated and put over the side — but decided against it. She simply did not want to appear before Bobby Morgan in that chic little two-piece outfit which revealed rather more than she had realized when she bought it. And so she lounged on deck, fighting back an urge to leave each time that some sleek launch or powerful runabout drew up to disembark a new group of gay arrivals.

She was being silly, she kept telling herself. Here were people whose names and faces she recognized from the social pages of the newspapers. People with a background of wealth and position to uphold. People accustomed to the prying watchfulness of public curiosity concerning everything they did. They were, she tried to believe, simply over-reacting to the unaccustomed release from that strict world of publicity, where their every move was observed and judged by a prejudiced jury of newspaper columnists whose livelihood depended on the production of scandal, of envious critics from a lower rung on the social ladder, blue-nosed reformers whose only thought was to condemn, radicals dedicated to the indiscriminate destruction of all who profited under a system which their twisted minds hated.

Bobby was attentive — too attentive for Betty's peace of mind. When he was not busy greeting friends in that whimsically charming manner which he seemed to turn on and off at will, he stayed close by her side, now telling some amusing anecdote about this or that well-known figure, casually introducing celebrities by their first names, and always quietly pressing her to drink. She was glad when he suggested a game of shuffleboard, for it offered some outlet for the tension which was gathering within her.

She learned quickly and played well. Too well, as she was to see shortly. Her reflexes were needle-sharp, her supple body under perfect control. Bobby, she soon noticed, seemed to tire quickly. The tanned aura of well-being and good health was but a facade. Years of dissipation had sapped his energy and staying-power, jangled his coordination. He was capable of brief, brilliant flashes of nervous effort, but he was no match for Betty's sure and confident precision. Finally he conceded the game and, leaving her rather abruptly, he joined a group of newcomers.

A tall, languorous redhead, stretched on a deck chair, turned lazily toward Betty as she found a place on the side lines.

"Bad tactics, my dear," she murmured.

"I'm afraid I don't understand," said Betty, her brow wrinkling with puzzlement.

"You're Bobby's new one, I take it," the other girl stated, rather than asked. She took off her sun glasses and offered a cigaret. "I seem to remember that I was Bobby's new one once. But it also seems like a long time ago now, and I won't be cutting my own throat if I give you a little tip. Bobby doesn't like to lose. You're not supposed to win if you play with Bobby."

"Why how absurd!" Betty exclaimed. "It was only a silly game."

The other pouted her crimsoned lips and blew a series of tiny smoke patterns which the wind carried away.

"Silly to you, perhaps," she amended, "but not to Bobby. No game is silly enough for Bobby to lose gracefully. I take it that you don't know Bobby too well — yet. Well, I do. I know what happens if you don't let Bobby win. Somehow, someday when you least expect it, he exacts a sudden, final revenge."

Betty said nothing, turning this new revelation over in her mind. The other girl smiled as though at some private, bitter joke, and then went on.

"I made the same mistake when I first knew him, when I was dancing at the Caper House. I thought a lot of things were just games then. And I didn't always let Bobby win. Well, I learned. I learned by finding out that there wasn't a club in town that would hire me after Bobby passed the word around. I learned by discovering that the people he'd introduced me to suddenly didn't know me any more. I learned by finding every door closed to me in the only thing I do well — dancing. And I ended up by crawling back to him on my hands and knees, like a whipped pup, begging him to let me shine his shoes or something. If you think I'm exaggerating, you simply don't know Bobby Morgan."

Betty studied the girl's profile. There was something familiar about that too-wise face, but it took her several minutes to place it. Then something clicked into place.

"You're Janet Castle, aren't you?" she asked.

"Taking a well-earned rest," the other agreed, "after a ten-month run in *Doll Babies*. And saying more than I should, probably."

"I see," said Betty. "Thank you."

She went to her cabin to dress for dinner.

Dinner was served on deck — an exquisite Continental meal prepared by a chef Bobby had lured away from an internationally known French hotel. His pique over the outcome of the shuffle board game apparently forgotten, Bobby sat next to her at a small table which accommodated six. His gay wit frolicked cleverly back and forth as he carefully chose for Betty from the seemingly numberless dishes which were offered. A truffled squab called forth a reference to Brillat-Savarin, who Betty remembered vaguely as being a well-known gourmet of the eighteenth century. Tiny oyster-crabs had already brought about a discussion of the position of Antoine's in New Orleans in the general scheme of *gourmandise.* Occasionally, as Bobby talked, his hand sought Betty's and pressed it, as though for some point he was making. At such times, although her first impulse was to snatch it away, Betty let her hand lie quietly until some pretext for a seemingly natural disentanglement offered itself. And always, it seemed, Bobby was refilling her glass or urging her to finish the last one. Pink champagne, now, which she rather liked, although not in the quantity which Bobby pressed upon her.

Later, after the tables were whisked away, strings of Chinese lanterns twinkled like fireflies in the gathering dark, and under their magic light people danced to a small orchestra hired for those last few hours before sailing time. Betty danced first with Bobby, then with a succession of young men to whom she had been introduced.

At last she excused herself from the attentions of an admiring young architect and made her way to the bow of the boat where she could be alone. She leaned over the rail, watching the shimmering lights reflected in the black water, humming along with the orchestra as a nostalgic melody echoed off to shore. She felt a bit giddy, and knew that she had allowed Bobby to fill her glass just once too often. She would be more careful of that in the future, she decided. More careful about everything until the next few days were over.

This was her big chance, Rocky had said. She laughed silently. Her big chance to what? To become another Janet Castle? To go down that same bitter road which twisted in every direction but the right one? No — what she must do was to let Bobby grow bored with her without offending him. The notion of deliberate planning in such a matter repelled her, but she knew she must do it. Find the delicate line of balance between outright rudeness and implicit acceptance, and tread it carefully —

"Oh, *here* you are!"

It was Bobby, swaying ever so slightly more than the roll of the sea made necessary.

"Running off from us, eh? Playing puss-in-the-corner?"

"Not at all." Betty's laugh was thin. "It's just so lovely out here … I wanted to be alone for a few minutes."

"Fine. I approve of being alone. Especially when there are two to be alone."

Bobby's cigarette lighter flared momentarily, and Betty caught a glimpse of his face. He *was* handsome, in a tired way that was at once older and younger than his actual age. He settled himself next to her and flicked ashes into the sea.

"It's a funny thing," he said. "I go off on one of these damn cruises and end up without ever having seen the places I've been. Just as I haven't had a chance to be alone with you, to get to know you. But we'll have a week — seven long nights — to change that.

"I've never been on a yacht before," Betty said, trying to veer the conversation away from the channel where Bobby appeared to be steering it. "Everything is new to me, and a bit — fantastic."

Bobby lurched against her. His breath curled warmly on her neck as his lips sought her shoulder.

"I'm sure we'll both enjoy it," he said.

Betty squirmed in his embrace, but before she could even voice a protest, an outside interruption freed her. She drew away as Bobby turned toward the voice which called his name.

"Hey Bobby! What about that movie?" someone asked. "They don't want to start it until you give the word."

"Movie? Oh yes. We'll be right there." He took Betty's arm. "A sort of preview *before* the previews," he explained. "Ruth Seavers' latest. Nat Brophy flew a print in from the coast this afternoon."

Together they went to the lounge, where Betty watched the miracle of a large, modernistic painting slipping noiselessly aside to uncover a movie-screen. And there, for the length of time it took to run off a new cartoon and the Ruth Seavers feature, she was able to relax.

But as the screen finally went dark and the soft amber lights came up again, Betty found her problem still unsolved. Bobby insisted that she have another drink — bars, either permanent or portable, seemed to be almost the most important feature of the yacht — and then suggested that they go down to his cabin.

"There's so much racket here," he explained with a winning smile, "and I simply must hear Bill Towne's broadcast. A show I have an interest in opened last night, and somebody told me he was going to pan it over the air. I just want to see if he dares."

"You mean it really is a good show?" Betty asked absently. In her mind she was turning over the question of whether or not it might be better to speak alone with Bobby, tell him frankly that his attentions were unwelcome when they passed the point of mere friendliness, and ask that she be taken back to shore if that could not be firmly understood.

"I haven't the slightest idea," Bobby said. "The point is that Bill's 'Towne's Talk' column is syndicated by a newspaper service my family has owned for years. Bill should know better than to bite the hand that feeds him, but if not — well, he has a surprise in store for him."

He took the last of his drink in two gulps, and, over Betty's half-murmured protests, led her to the elaborate suite he reserved for himself.

A huge photo-mural of New York's dramatic skyline covered one entire wall, so cleverly lighted that, looking at it, it was difficult to realize that one was not in some towering Manhattan penthouse. But at the touch of a button this too slid away, revealing a glass-enclosed verandah, where the ever-changing moods of the sea and sky must paint for its occupant a vast canvas of Nature's own making.

Here Betty uneasily seated herself on a large, wine-colored couch, unconscious of the fact that its rich, vibrant tone formed a perfect setting for her own golden beauty. Bobby fiddled with the radio, and the strains of a hotel orchestra filled the verandah. He glanced at his watch, then came over to sit beside her.

"Don't you think, Betty," he asked, "that it's time you began to let your hair down and enjoy yourself?"

Betty tried to force gaiety into her laugh.

"I'm sorry if I've seemed rude," she said. "It's just as I told you. This is so new to me — so much like a Hollywood set — that I've hardly been able to believe it. You must remember that I'm just a drab little mouse from the other side of the tracks."

"Some things," Bobby said suggestively, "are the same on both sides of the tracks. For instance, has anyone ever told you that you have a gorgeous, wonderfully desireable body?"

Betty gasped, speechless at this direct approach. She started to rise, but Bobby's hand rested heavily on her arm.

"Well, you have. You can take the word of one who might be considered somewhat of a connoisseur of such things. I've known a lot of girls, Betty, but never one who was so deliciously, and unintentionally, exciting. I've been watching you all day — wanting you. Watching the unaffected way you walk, the easy, natural way you use your body. Thinking what a shame it is to keep all that loveliness hidden away from someone who could really appreciate it. Betty ... "

Suddenly his arms were about her. Before she could draw back, his mouth sought hers, his lips crushing savagely against her own. She felt his tongue slip moistly across the bruised cupid's bow, probing snakelike, probing .... One hot palm moved across her shoulder ...

"Don't!" Betty half-sobbed in the only voice she could summon from her fear gripped throat. "Oh please, *please!*"

Something in her pleading seemed to arouse him even more. He flung his weight against her, forcing her backward into the pillows. His knee pressed sharply upon her, and now his fingers gripped a shoulder brutally. Into her ear his lust-thick voice murmured hideously, using words which she had learned to hate, words which were full of false love, vile pleadings. She felt her senses swimming, and knew that she was close to a half-fainting helplessness. Knew that if she could not fight off the blackness every word of that frenzied filth would become a hellish reality.

She heard the seams of her dress tear as Bobby fought for her breasts.

"I'll buy you a dozen new ones," he promised hoarsely. "We don't have time for snaps and fastners."

From somewhere Betty summoned a final fury of strength Wrenching free, she thrust herself frantically from the couch and ran to the door. Bobby swore and lurched to his feet.

"Come back here, you little — " he commanded. "Where do you think you're going to go?"

Betty's only thought at that moment was to escape from the lush prison of Bobby's suite. Once outside, she turned blindly down a passage, in the direction where she thought her own cabin lay. Behind her Bobby's uncertain footsteps followed.

Somewhere, during those next awful minutes, she became completely confused. The cabin numbers were all wrong, and she realized that she was lost. Still she went on and on, praying for some miracle.

And there, suddenly, it was. Oh, a very minor miracle, perhaps, but safety for a while at least. An unoccupied cabin, the door invitingly open. She darted in and fastened the lock with mere seconds to spare.

CHAPTER THREE
ROMAN CIRCUS

OBBY!" The second voice outside the door was throatily feminine, bright with amused laughter. "Whatever are you sitting there for? You usually carry your liquor better than that."

Betty's heart leaped, and she strained to hear every word.

"I," said Bobby wryly, "am waiting for a friend. I frequently sit like this while I wait for friends. Sometimes I read a book."

"The racing-form, if I know you," said the woman. "And how does your friend feel about all this?"

"My friend," Bobby answered, "is acting very strangely. A touch of the vapours, or something equally mid-Victorian. You, of course, would know nothing about these matters, being — as I seem to recall from somewhere — anything but mid-Victorian."

"Let me see … Cannes, wasn't it?"

"Nice, the first time. Cannes was afterward, while you were between marriages. Or was it between divorces? Something dull and domestic."

"Perhaps we should find some quiet spot and try to remember. Remembrance is a very important part of *l'amour,* I've heard."

"I'm sure you could refresh my memory very quickly."

"I have a dandy little memory course … "

There was a moment — a long moment — of silence, punctuated by a soft feline moan. An alley-cat, Betty thought, making promises on a back fence.

"Darling," Bobby said, "It begins to come back to me now. Let's dash back to my hovel and start our homework. I promised myself I'd catch Towne's broadcast anyway, and reception is very bad right here. I'm not getting a thing."

"And your — friend?"

"I'll make another appointment sometime."

The voices faded down the corridor. Betty was alone. Her first instinct was to collapse with relief, but she shook it off. This was her chance — perhaps her only chance, for there was no knowing when Bobby might erratically decide to return. Somehow she had to get out on deck and make a break for shore. She didn't dare take time to find her own cabin and swim suit. Perhaps here, in one of the closets or drawers …

But a hurried search revealed nothing. Worse — some over-efficient attendant had cleaned the room so scrupulously that she could not even find a pin, and her dress, in its present condition, was impossible. Torn to the waist, it fell away in revealing folds in such a way that she could not even hold it together decently. Besides, if Bobby happened to come across her before she got into the water, she wasn't going to take time to struggle with a dress before going over the side.

She made up her mind. She'd strip down to her slip, try to come up on deck somewhere forward where it was deserted, and disappear before anyone saw her. That was the theory of it, anyway. Rapidly she slipped her dress over her head, kicked off her slippers, and peeled her sheer hose away. Her bra needed repairs so badly that she wriggled out of it.

At that moment she caught sight of herself once more in the paneled mirror. Tousled blonde hair on a head habitually carried with a proud, fearless lilt. Eyes almost violet in their blueness, wide apart and steady. A nose that showed an exasperating tendency to turn upward at the tip, undecided whether to be classic or cute. Lips that were full without slackness, lips that smiled a lot.

Betty had never felt shame in her own body. She was natural and honest in her understanding of that body's sleeping, fecund mystery. Someday, she had always known, she would meet a man whose quiet tenderness would awaken all her femaleness. But now, after tonight, could she still feel that way? Bobby's touch made her feel dirty, and she welcomed the thought of the cleansing sea.

Nothing had changed, she told herself. Nothing must be allowed to change — she owed that to the love which would someday come into her life. But what if — what if *all* sex was like that? Oh, it wasn't! She knew too many decent young men. had been friends with them, talked with them, romped with them on the beach —

She yanked herself out of that brief reverie. No time to think now. She must act. She unlocked the door and peeped down the corridor. It was deserted. She stepped out and stole along catlike, her bare feet soundless on the deep-piled carpeting.

She hurried around a corner — and walked directly into the arms of a man who was coming the opposite way. She felt the rough texture of his jacket on her bare skin, felt the large, capable hands take her upper arms and thrust her rather firmly away. Gray eyes that smouldered, flecked by specks of amber, stared at her without expression. Then something like contempt touched the corner of his wide, tensed mouth. His hands released her, and he stepped aside.

"I — beg your pardon," Betty choked. Her cheeks were burning, and she knew she was blushing furiously. She moved past him, and in the narrowness of the passage her hip brushed lightly against him. Knowing that he was looking after her, that those clear eyes could not help but be drawn to the pert swinging of her rounded hips, she hurried on. He had not spoken a word.

Sooner than she had dared hope, Betty found a small, spiraling iron stairway that led to the deck. And here she was in luck again, for it let her out far forward, in a dark corner beside a ventilating funnel. She glanced this way and that, saw no one who was looking in that direction, and scurried swiftly to the rail. It was the act of an instant to swing over it, then hang poised while she gauged the long drop to the water. She arched forward, thrusting outward as far as she could, dropped like a plummet and cut the surface cleanly.

The chill of the water shocked her into almost instantaneous motion, and she was swimming strongly even as she came up again. She struck out for shore, but had gone no more than a dozen strokes before a voice cut the night like a knife.

"Man over! Man overboard!"

Other voices rose excitedly as the passengers and crew rushed to the side. Betty could have cried with frustration. They'd lower a boat, come after her — Well, let them! She'd fight them until she was dead; she'd force herself under and drown! Grimly she swam on, her feet thrashing the water to foam as she strove to widen the gap between herself and the yacht.

A powerful searchlight began to play over the water, finally picked out her half-nude body in its pitiless glare.

"Whee!" a drunken voice exclaimed. "Better have your glasses examined, sailor. That's no man, unless they've changed the model recently."

"And hardly drowning, I'd say. That girl knows where she's going, and she's in a hurry."

Within moments she heard Bobby, inquiring, anxious. Then he laughed.

"Shall we put a boat out, sir?" an officer asked.

"Not on your life," Bobby said. "Anybody who doesn't like my parties is always free to leave. It's an easy swim for her, especially with the tide. Keep the spot on her, though, just to be sure. Besides, it's more fun that way." He laughed again, and there was an answering chorus.

"I'm just wondering," he called across the water, "what plans you have for your arrival. Going to hail a bus in that outfit?"

Betty set her teeth. This was their idea of sport — playing a spotlight on an almost-naked, humiliated girl while they taunted her with her helplessness, reminded her of further humiliation to come. The Roman Circus again.

She swam on and on, until the voices blurred and the laughter faded. Somewhere her brassiere, none-too-securely patched, slipped away. The spotlight followed her in until it was obvious that she was safe in the shallows, then died out. Some one of Bobby's sailors, evidently, had enough decency to let her make shore under cover of darkness. Even that seemed like a lot when she considered the sort of values she had seen that night.

CHAPTER FOUR
BARE ESCAPE

As she waded to shore, Betty instinctively chose a rocky stretch of beach which she knew was commonly avoided. Picking her way along the shell-strewn sand, she stayed close in the shadow of the huge boulders which frowned out agelessly at the restless Atlantic. The night was warm, and, after her chilling swim, she was almost as grateful for that as for its amicable blackness. The problem of getting home had just begun.

If only she could find some empty cottage, some unused fishing shanty — anything where she might scavenge a few scraps of clothing! But how to tell, at this hour, if a darkened window really meant that no one was inside? Never had she sensed so strongly the vast unfriendliness of the world outside herself. She thought of her waiting apartment, the cozy chair where she so often curled up with the companionship of a book, the friendly door now within easy walking distance — and so unapproachable, so far ...

The night wind blew caressingly over her shoulders, and she felt the briny droplets drying stickily on her skin. Her hands impatiently sought her body, brushing away the invisible settling of salt which clung to it. Crab grass grasped at her ankles as she reached the dunes and moved cautiously along them. Then, just as she topped the summit of the first ridge, the moon, so discreetly hidden before, pushed from behind a bank of clouds. Silhouetted against the skyline, Betty felt that no moon had ever shone with more revealing intensity. She broke into a run, racing for the shadows of the beginning line of trees.

What she at first took to be a cabin loomed out before her. Then she realized that it was a trailer, standing in such a way as to almost hide the powerful-looking open car to which it was hitched. It was dark, and from the protection of a huge tree's gloom, Betty thoughtfully studied it.

At last she picked up a dozen pebbles and weighed them in her hand. There was one way of finding out if the trailer was occupied and still not give herself away completely. The pebbles rattled loudly on the metal roof as she tossed them.

Nothing happened. She tried another handful, and another. Then, still cautious, she stole softly to its hulking side and listened breathlessly for some sound within. Moments later she tried the door-latch. It was unlocked, and the door swung soundlessly open. On tiptoe she stepped apprehensively inside. Moonlight lay in jagged patches where it fell through the windows, and a quick glance told Betty that the trailer was deserted.

She felt no qualms about what she now must do. The simplest necessities were all she asked, and she had, of course, no intention of keeping them. In the morning a messenger could be sent over with an anonymous bundle and a note of thanks for an unauthorized loan which could not be explained. If the trailer was gone by then, she could easily trace its ownership by the license plates.

Her eyes swept the tidy interior for the most likely storage place for clothing. With space at a minimum, clever designing had offered a surprising number of possibilities. A flashlight, held by a spring-clamp on the wall of the miniature galley, offered some assistance in the search. Betty did not know if the regular lights would work without the usual trailer-park connection, and at any rate she would not have dared risk them.

But now a bitter disappointment awaited her. Every drawer, every cabinet, proved to be locked. Even the kitchen utensils, from which she might have taken a sturdy knife to jimmy a lock or remove a set of hinges, were securely put away. Only one door was open — that which opened on the little lavatory and shower. Here Betty found the only thing that looked promising.

Towels. Not skimpy, economical things, scaled to the size of the racks they hung upon. Huge woolly ones, as big as bathmats. Betty snatched at them desperately.

Another thought came to her. The couch. Since it was used for sleeping purposes, it must have a layer of blankets under a top spread. With a blanket thrown over her shoulders, a towel draped carelessly about her neck, she could pass for a member of some late swimming party. A pair of towels beneath would do for a swimming suit. In such an outfit she could move about relatively freely until she found a better solution to her dilemma.

With her hand on the towels, she looked longingly at the shower. Her hair felt gummy from the sea. Her whole body was uncomfortable under its dusting of salt. She tried the faucet and found that the shower evidently had its own reservoir. Did she dare? It would take only a moment...

She stepped under the cool spray and rapidly washed her hair clean, let the fresh water pour over her for the few seconds it took to carry away the sea sediment. Then she wrung out her panties and hung them over the wash-bowl. She knew they would have no time to dry, but at least she would not leave wet marks about the place while she pieced together her improvised wardrobe.

The last idea struck her as being rather ridiculous. She giggled quickly as she pulled back the spread of the couch. She pictured herself as a bride-to-be, working over a trousseau made up of bath towels and army blankets. The pent-up reaction to all that had happened began to trickle through the dam of her enforced calm. She laughed, and went on laughing, surprised that she could not stop. Then overwhelming hysteria seized her. She flung herself, naked, on the couch, buried her face in the pillows, and alternately sobbed and giggled, beating her doubled fists into the blankets. Tears poured down her cheeks as the paroxysm racked her, wore itself away.

Eventually she lay quietly gasping, not yet in complete control of herself, but too exhausted to go on. A violent chill ran through her, and she weakly drew a blanket over her shivering flesh.

Within minutes she was deeply, dreamlessly, asleep.

CHAPTER FIVE
STRIP TEASE

A n irregular, rocking sensation brought Betty slowly to consciousness. For a moment the movement, coupled with the neat economy of the space about her, led her to believe that she was somehow back on the yacht, and she sat up in startled panic. But the gray light of false dawn, lining the trailer's interior, soon re-

The trailer was *moving!* She sprang from the couch and stared out the window at a landscape which was wholly unfamiliar. By the spicy tang of the chill air she guessed that she was somewhere in the mountains, and an occasional glimpse of the skyline soon bore this out. How long the trailer had been traveling she could not even guess; its direction, she decided after several minutes, was generally north.

Driven back to the couch by cold, she curled her arms around her knees and reflected on how best to cope with this unthought-of development. Since there was no window at the front end of the trailer, she could not even see who was in the car. Speculation was a matter of complete frustration. She was on her way *somewhere,* and that was all she could be sure of at the moment. She might draw some slight comfort from the thought that every turn of the wheels was taking her further away from Bobby Morgan and everything connected with him. That, at least, was something to be grateful for.

She dozed off into a fitful napping. Once or twice, half waking, she noticed that the road was no longer a smooth highway. It seemed to curve more frequently as it climbed, and twigs occasionally brushed the trailer sides as it passed some close-growing tree. A single Dali-like dream now began to thread through her slumber, recurring again and again, like a phrase in a cracked phonograph record. She was in a department store, trying to go up on an escalator which was going down. An enraged floor manager was pursuing her, and he was waving a black umbrella and shouting —

"What the devil's the idea of this?"

Betty jerked awake, shaking her head to drive the fog of sleep from her brain. Two angry gray eyes were boring into hers. She saw a wide mouth, set now in a fixed, hard line.

It was the man she had met in the passageway of the yacht.

"Get up out of there," he demanded, "and start explaining yourself. And," he added grimly, "it had better be good."

"I — can't get up," Betty said in a voice far from steady.

"Oh — a slight case of the jim-jams this morning? Perhaps you'd like breakfast in bed?" The mouth grew more tense, and Betty hastened to explain.

"I … I haven't any clothes on," she said.

"Haven't any — " His eyes searched the trailer in three seconds. "Nonsense. I don't know what your game is, but — " He tugged at the blankets as though to yank them from the couch. Betty grabbed them back, just a fraction of a second too late.

"All right," he said after a moment of frozen, astonished silence. "I was mistaken about that. Damn it, *put on* your clothes! Where did you hide them, anyway?"

"I haven't got any, except — except what's in the shower."

He reached the door in four gigantic strides and peered in. When he turned, his face was grimmer than ever, and a bit flushed.

"As I said," he began, "I don't know what you're trying to pull, but I know that I don't like it. I — wait a minute! You're the girl who ran into me on Morgan's yacht, aren't you? Evidently you make it a habit to run around half-naked. A confirmed nudist, perhaps?"

His sarcasm, the whole injustice of her situation, brought anger to Betty's eyes. And, with anger, she found her tongue.

"The way you saw me on that yacht," she said, "was an unfortunate necessity. Perhaps you heard that a girl swam home from that buggy-ride rather than accept the kind of hospitality Bobby Morgan offered her. Well, I was that girl, and I couldn't swim in what was left of my dinner dress. I lost my bra in the water, and I came in here looking for something to wear. Everything was locked up, and I was so exhausted that I fell asleep. Now, if you will lend me some old scraps that you were going to give to the Salvation Army anyway, I will be only too glad to leave your trailer and more of this cavalier treatment which seems to be a trademark of Bobby Morgan's friends."

The man sat down in a chair and studied her. Finally he shook his head.

"It sounds good, but it just doesn't jell. I heard that some girl jumped ship after a drunken brawl with Morgan, but that certainly doesn't win you your merit badge. No one who knows your crew is much surprised at anything that happens when they're loaded. Diving off a boat in the middle of the night, sneaking naked into the trailer of a man they know is going off for a week in the mountains, is just the sort of thing your bunch thinks is cute. Especially when the intended victim of the little joke is someone who won't play their kind of game, someone who has never been at pains to conceal just how cheap ... and rotten ... and generally worthless ... he knows them to be. Tell me, was this your idea, or did Bobby put you up to it?"

"You're forgetting one thing!" Betty cried. "If I was on that yacht, so were you! Don't you think it's possible that I may feel the same way about them that you *say* you do? I was there only because Rocky — you know the Deep Sea Club? — because Rocky made it almost a part of my job."

"In that case," he said, "it begins to sound like something worse."

Betty's cheeks flamed under the sting of his quiet misinterpretation of her explanation.

"Would you mind telling me," she said coldly, "how you reconcile this holier-than-thou attitude with the fact that *you* attend his parties?"

The hard face darkened. "I was — looking for someone. I was not there by invitation, although I was invited to leave. But there's no point in continuing this. I stopped so I could get a pack of cigarettes out of here. I'll take them and leave you the keys so you can find something to wear. The road isn't so bad that you can't make breakfast — if you know how. I've got another two hours' drive ahead of me."

"What town will that be?"

"Town? There isn't any town. This is the heart of the Maine woods."

"Maine? But — how am I to get back to Long Island?"

"I don't know. You might walk. Or perhaps you can find a river and swim."

"You can't *do* this!" Betty exclaimed. "You'll have to drive me somewhere so I can wire for my fare back."

"I don't have to do anything for you, young lady. Especially if it means missing a day of the first week off I've had in a year. Time is too precious for me to waste the way you and your playmates do. You may have thought that at this point I'd do almost anything to be rid of you, that I'd put you on a train with a bribe and a ticket, so you could run back to town with your charming little anecdote. Well, the joke has back-fired. I'm going on with what I started out to do. I suppose I ought to let you live on nuts and berries while we're up here, but I'll see that you're adequately fed as well as clothed. For one week. Then I'll drop you as I found you — well, perhaps not *exactly* as I found you — and you can shout the big adventure from the roof-tops if you want to."

Betty's nails dug her palms, but she smothered her anger deeply enough to make her voice frigid.

"There is a law against kidnapping," she said.

"I refuse to be blackmailed. Try it."

"My job — "

"If this doubtful job — and you — are both as you represent them, I shouldn't think you'd want it. Besides, weren't you starting out for a week's cruise?"

"And exactly what are people to think about my being up here in the woods with you"

"If you must tell them, much the same thing as they would think about you being a week on the water with Bobby Morgan."

He opened a drawer, took out cigarettes, and tossed the keys to the couch. He paused at the door to take one long, searching look at her, then slammed it decisively. An instant later the trailer jolted into motion.

CHAPTER SIX

TEMPTATION

For several minutes Betty sat in the pile of rumpled bedclothes, arms folded belligerently across her chest, and wrestled with her anger. It seemed to her that the whole world was in unfair conspiracy against her and, far from accepting defeat, she was prepared to take up arms and do battle against the fates themselves. Through no fault of her own — unless her original weakness in following Rocky's order be so named — she had found herself in one untenable position after another, and her spirit was in complete revolt to take up arms and do battle against the fates themselves. Through no fault of her own — unless her original weakness in following Rocky, Bobby Morgan, and now this smug-sounding stranger — all of them, in their own ways, had been pushing her around. She wasn't going to be pushed around any longer.

She picked up the bunched keys which had been tossed onto the blankets, rattled them angrily in her hand, and thrust one bare leg tentatively out to test the chill of the air, as a hesitant swimmer toes the water. Then, with a sudden motion, she flung the covers back and sprang lightly to her feet. Naked, unconsciously swaying with the rocking of the trailer, she opened drawers and closets, rummaging for something to wear.

When it was complete, the outfit she put together was not exactly the sort of thing one wore to cocktails at the Rainbow Room. Patched dungarees that were too long in the legs, too large in the waist, and too tight at the hips. A faded blue shirt that didn't fit in any direction, and a pull-over sweater which sagged alarmingly where it should have snuggled. Long wool socks which came above her knees. The shoes she had found were of a size which gave her the feeling that she was wearing skis.

The business of making breakfast presented a further problem. Her host, if he could be called that, had suggested that it was possible to cook while the trailer was in motion, but it seemed a somewhat risky undertaking. She got as far as starting coffee, guarding the pot warily, when the trailer slowed and swung gently into a clearing beside the road. She heard the car door slam, and then came a firm rap on the trailer door. She called out, and the bulk of the young man towered into the room.

"I decided to have some breakfast," he announced. He looked at the odd assortment of clothing Betty wore, and the corners of his mouth twitched.

"I believe you'll find a comb and a couple of new toothbrushes in that top left drawer." He turned his back and busied himself in the kitchenette. "Can you fry an egg?" he asked from somewhere in the refrigerator.

"Yes, I can fry an egg," Betty said, her voice dripping acid.

"I will have three. Once over lightly. But *lightly.* And bacon. And fruit juice. Toast crisp, not just bread with a sunburn."

"Now see here." The line of Betty's jaw jutted sharply. "This whole ridiculous affair has gone far enough. I don't want to be here, and I don't intend to stay. Do you still refuse to drive me to a town?"

"I do."

"Then I'll have to hitchhike."

"And when you get to a town?"

"I'll — I'll manage." She had been about to say that she would wire for money, but suddenly she realized that she knew no one of whom she wanted to ask such a favor — with its attendant complicating explanations. "And I'll want to return your things, so if you'll tell me who you are ... "

"Donald Hammond — as though you didn't know. Look in the Westchester phone book. But please don't use my name as a reference when the police pick you up. They're going to be very much interested in what you're up to, bumming around the country looking like that. But don't let me keep you. I think I hear a car coming now — and they're mighty scarce up here."

He thrust a comb into her hand and opened the trailer door. Betty stumbled out and hurried clumsily across the road. Within moments an ancient, mobile wreck rocked into sight, bearing two youths of college age. Betty watched anxiously as it slowed to a crawl.

"Good God! What is it?" she heard one of them yell over the gasping engine.

"I dunno. All kinds of things sprout up along the roads."

"Maybe we ought to pick it up for laughs."

"Maybe we better not. It probably isn't housebroken, and its pappy has a shotgun."

The car chugged slowly past, then picked up speed. Cheeks aflame, Betty hobbled a few steps farther down the road. Time passed, and silence fell, broken by the morning calls of birds and a happy-sounding basso which rumbled from the trailer, along with a businesslike rattling of pans and dishes. Soon a tantalizing odor of frying bacon wafted on a fitful breeze, along with the pungent promise of the coffee which she had been making. Betty's stomach questioned, and she began to wonder how long it would be before she had a meal again. A long time, she decided, if she were to depend on the helpfulness of Donald Hammond — whoever he was.

And then she knew who he was. An article in a news-weekly had carried a picture of him recently. She remembered, because he didn't look like the type you expected to be doing nuclear research. He looked like a football player, or an oarsman — both of which he had been. As for his family — everybody had heard of the Hammonds. It was one of the names you grew up knowing, like the Cabots and the Lodges. Stacked up beside the Hammonds, Bobby Morgan was something like poor white trash. But Donald wasn't cashing in on the family name. Instead of moving into the executive end of his father's manufacturing business, he was working in a laboratory for less than his father paid a good machinist. And that, Betty thought, pointed up the only thing money was good for. If you had enough of it to begin with, you could often do more useful work than you might have done if you'd gone chasing dollars.

The hum of another car brought her attention back to her own immediate predicament. She thought it might help if she gave the appearance of walking, so she started down the highway. The car approached swiftly, and she saw that it was an open sports model with a girl at the wheel and a somewhat too-much-older man beside her. Betty raised her thumb in a half-hearted gesture. Unexpectedly, the car screeched to a sudden stop a few yards past her. She trotted toward it. The man was lighting a cigarette for the girl, and as Betty reached the car the girl blew a long, billowing cloud of smoke and amusedly eyed her.

"Tired of walking?" the girl asked.

"Well — " Betty was about to admit that she hadn't done any walking yet, when the girl slipped the car into gear.

"Run awhile," the girl suggested, and the car leaped forward. The girl waved cheerily as Betty stared after it.

This was too much. Slowly, Betty walked back to the trailer and rapped at the door.

"Forget something?" Donald Hammond asked as she entered. In her absence he had changed his clothes for rough woods-togs.

"Very funny. You were probably watching."

"As a matter of fact, I was. I wanted to observe your technique."

"May I have some breakfast?"

"Certainly, if you make it." He poured himself a second cup of coffee, and watched her at work. "You look better with your hair combed," he said.

Betty set a place for herself at the folding wall-table and deftly flipped the two eggs she was frying. Once over — lightly. She made the toast dark and crisp, and the bacon was not allowed to shrivel away. She ate a few mouthfuls in silence, and then said,

"I'm afraid you're stuck with me."

"You get an 'A' for effort, anyway. But now, since we'll apparently be living together for the next several days, don't you think I

should know *your* name? I can't just yell, 'Hey, you!' every time there's wood to be chopped or a mess of dishes to be washed."

"I'm Betty Brooks, and if you think I am going to be yelled 'Hey' anything, you are going to end up with an awful pile of dirty dishes."

"Don't work, and you don't eat. Remember, I didn't invite you on this trip."

"Fair enough. But don't *you* forget that I didn't plan to come along."

"Still sticking with that story, hmm?"

"I haven't thought of a less improbable one yet."

"I thought it was pretty clumsy myself."

"Mr. Hammond, I have told you exactly how I came to fall asleep in your trailer. I am beginning not to care much whether or not you believe me. Since we will be in each other's hair anyway, I suggest that we stop discussing it. I'll try to do my share of whatever work is to be done, and I'll stay out of your way as much as possible. Will that be satisfactory?"

"A bargain. When you've finished your coffee, perhaps you'd like to ride up front, so you can see where you're going for a change. Put on another pair of heavy socks, and those shoes will come closer to fitting you."

For the next couple of hours Betty drank in the heavy morning air and watched the landscape slide quickly by as they drove into country which was even wilder and more sparsely settled. Conversation, at first rather warily polite, gradually became more relaxed, and before they arrived at their destination Betty realized that under skillful, casual questioning, she had related to Donald Hammond what amounted to a brief, but quite complete, history of her life.

CHAPTER SEVEN
FRESH LIPSTICK

THE road, which had narrowed to a single corrugated-log lane, twisted through the woods beside a stream and finally ended in a cleared knoll which, on one side, sloped down a grassy bank to a pebbled flat, beyond which the water tumbled and sparkled in a wide curve. The second open side faced on a small, crystal-clear pool which lay, jewel-like and placid, under the reflected sky. The remainder of the clearing was irregularly bounded by virgin forest.

"It's — a beautiful place," Betty said as she stepped out of the car and tried to look at everything at once. "But where is it? In case I get lost and have to ask directions."

Don grinned. "Up here you ask directions of a compass, and if you get lost you stay lost. It's a timber tract belonging to — well, my father turned it over to me a few years ago. Somebody once started to log it, but got no further than building the road."

He unhitched the trailer and drew the car a few feet away from it, then went about setting up camp. With a sickle he quickly cleared away what brush had sprung up on the site, introduced Betty to the mysteries of the permanent fireplace which he had built, then led her to a nearby spring for drinking water, pointing out the blaze marks, which, he explained, would indicate, on any trails in the vicinity, whether one was headed toward camp or away from it. Finally he gave her a pocket compass and a whistle.

"Now," he said, "short of putting you on a leash, I've done all I can to keep you out of trouble. There's just one thing more."

They went into the trailer, where he took two revolvers from the gun cabinet.

"Have you ever fired one of these things?"

"I've done a little target shooting with my father," Betty said.

"Good. I'm leaving the .38 in this drawer. Loaded. You'll have no occasion to use it. But it's there if you need it."

He slipped the other, a .32, into a shoulder holster. Then he gathered his fishing tackle and put on waders.

"I'm going out to get lunch," he said. "You can tag along if you want to."

"I don't have to stay and chop wood?"

"Not this time," he grinned.

They did not go far. Don approached the little pool from its lower end, studied the edges of the water, and tied a gaudy dry fly to his line. Betty settled herself in a shaded spot and watched as he cast a dozen times with no result, and with no apparent loss of patience.

"Maybe the fish don't know what they are supposed to do," she suggested. "It's been so long since you've been here."

Don glowered her into silence, clipped the fly from the thin leader, and tried another, more somber, pattern. He false-cast a time or two, then laid the fly delicately beside an overhanging rock. Scarcely had it touched the surface when the water exploded in a flashing swirl.

For the next several minutes the outcome of the contest was uncertain, as the fortunes of battle favored first one side and then the other. But by degrees the fish tired, the startling runs became less spectacularly strong. Playing the line with his left hand, Don moved further into the water and readied his net as the trout changed its tactics and worked for a slack line and a loose hook. Foot by foot, and finally inch by inch, he brought it within netting reach. Rod bowed in a slim arc over his head, the man worked the trout into position. Then, suddenly, the line was limp and a plump, beautifully colored body wriggled in the throat of the landing net.

For a moment Don held the rainbow-streaked form in one hand, testing its heavy weight. Then, with one smart rap of a thin stick, he killed it cleanly. Within seconds it had been gutted and washed, after which he wrapped it in dampened moss and packed it in his creel.

"And is that," Betty asked, "what you drove all the way up here to do?"

"Yes, partly."

"Then, now that you've done it, you can turn around and go back again?"

Don had been switching the line in the air, drying the fly preparatory to casting again. He stopped.

"I think it's the silliest thing I've ever seen — a grown man driving hundreds of miles to kill fish," Betty continued.

Don sat down.

"The object," he said slowly, "is not to kill them, particularly, except when I plan to eat them. I have been on very successful fishing trips where I never came even close to catching anything. But I don't believe I could make a person like you understand exactly why I *do* go fishing."

"It's so *sporting*," Betty mocked. "A man weighing close to two hundred pounds locked in grim battle with a little thing like that. All sorts of fancy equipment pitted against a fish who is probably considered a bad sport if he manages to chew the line intwo."

Don passed the rod to her and slipped the net from the harness.

"Suppose you catch your own lunch," he suggested. "Not *pour le sport,* but simply to provide yourself with something to eat. You've seen how easy it is. But let me warn you first — this tackle is so light that you can't horse a fish out of the water with it. The hook on the fly is barbless, the intention being to free the fish without injury if you don't want to keep him — which means also that if you slack your line he will get rid of it in a hurry. All right, go to it."

Betty took the rod and stepped out on a jutting boulder.

"By the way," Don offered mildly, "you might as well get rid of that handkerchief you were carrying. You've ripped it to shreds."

For the first time Betty realized that at some time while she watched Don playing the fish, she had leaped to her feet and, all unconsciously, had torn to bits the handkerchief with which she had started to mop her brow.

Holding the bamboo as she had seen Don use it, Betty whipped it back and forth over her head. Then she threw forward strongly — and nothing happened. The fly had tangled in an overhanging branch behind her. She freed it and tried again, being careful not to hook the tree again. The fly jerked out a few feet, swung back in a tangle as the reel backlashed, and caught in her sweater, while the tip of the rod splashed the water at her feet.

"Of course," Don said smoothly, "it may take you a few minutes to get the hang of it. And I probably make you nervous. So I'll go back and do a few chores while you take care of the production department."

Betty said nothing. She was busy trying to untangle the line.

"If you decide that it isn't worth the effort," Don said as he rose and lazily stretched, "a can of beans is good, nourishing food."

He left her alone, and she could hear his soft, abstracted whistling as he busied himself around the campsite.

An hour and a half later Betty walked back to the clearing and handed him the rod.

"I lost the fly on a snag," she said. "I'm sorry."

She marched to the trailer and the door slammed. Neither she nor Don had mentioned the fact that she was wet to the waist as a result of having slipped into the pond.

Shortly the trailer door opened and Betty stuck her head out. She held a red and white can of beans in one hand.

"Where," she asked, "is the can opener?"

CHAPTER EIGHT
PRISONER OF LOVE

F ORTUNATELY, Don's trout, broiled with strips of bacon under a blanket of sassafras leaves, was ample for two — or he pretended that it was — so Betty's sentence to a diet of beans was suspended. Baked potatoes, fluffed biscuits hot from the reflector tin, and the strongest coffee she had ever tasted helped make the noonday meal one which, for all its simplicity, she was never to forget. Later she was to find that Don's camp cooking could be ingenious as well as satisfying.

He had set a black iron pot into one corner of the fireplace, where, bedded by coals, it was to simmer a perpetual stew for the remainder of their stay. Enriched and thickened by the addition of everything from small game to the meat of a large turtle, a cup of that ever-changing broth filled many places on the menu. With the addition of mussels from a sluggish pond it became a sort of chowder; with a brace of game birds added, it made the filling for a crusty pot-pie. From it, Betty thought, Bobby Morgan's imported chef could have learned a great measure of respect for the common stew.

But more impressive to her was Don's ability to produce food from sources which she had never considered. There were crayfish to be found, and, cooked like shrimps, they were delicious. For salads there were wild leeks, chicory and violets, the shoots of wild grape, watercress, and a dozen other greens. As cooking vegetables there were the tender fiddleheads of ferns, cowslips, dandelion, burdock,and even young milkweed. There were mushrooms, of course, and a heaping dish of frogs' legs which would have delighted a dinner at Rector's was the simple result of a little searching. In time Betty was to wonder how anyone ever managed to starve in the woods.

They ate their first meal at a rough plank table which Don had hammered together, and when they were finished he thumbnailed a splinter from it to frankly pick a fishbone from his teeth.

"The dishes are beginning to pile up on us," he observed. "Since you don't care for fishing, perhaps you'd take care of them if I leave you for the afternoon?"

"I'm quite willing to do whatever I can to earn my keep," Betty said.

"There's a pool on a branch a few miles up," Don said, "where an old enemy of mine hangs out. If he's getting stupid with age, I may be able to hook him."

As Don, a short time later, disappeared quietly into the woods, Betty sighed with the sheer relief of finding herself alone. For the first time since accepting Bobby Morgan's yachting invitation, she was able to relax and give some thought to her next move. Automatically she heated a kettle of water and cleared the table, but her mind was busy elsewhere.

When she had finished the few dishes, Betty sat on a bench, frowning over her own thoughts. At last she got up and slowly walked to the car. The key was in the ignition switch. She stepped in, and the motor soon purred into life. She sat there for several minutes more, then put the car in gear and turned it around. It moved so easily out onto the narrow log road — and ahead lay the freedom of the open highway and home.

The road was difficult, and she drove slowly — but as the moments went by, her pace dropped far below that made necessary by considerations of safety. It was a dirty trick which she was pulling and she knew it, although she told herself that it was no more inconsiderate than Don's refusal to help her get home, and that he was, in a sense, keeping hex a prisoner. She was quite certain that he could get along very well for a few days until she devised some way of getting the car back to take the trailer out. But at the same time she had to admit that he had been fair, considering all the circumstances. When she reached the junction of the road, the car was moving at a snail-like crawl.

She turned onto the wider road — and stopped. A voice within her urged her onward, away from the all-too-uncertain possibilities inherent in spending a week with a stranger. But —

"I can't do it to him," she said aloud. "I just can't do it — damn it."

"Well, kid," she told herself as she parked the car exactly where she had found it, "you had your chance. Whatever happens now is on your own head."

She spun the wheel and headed briskly back to the camp.

She decided to do something about her wardrobe. Not, of course, for Don's benefit. For her own comfort, and the possibility that she might have to travel part of the way home by train or bus. In the trailer, hunting needle and thread, she came across a pair of dungarees in even worse shape than the ones she had on — but which would make a perfectly good pair of camp shorts. Only — was it wise to make herself attractive in that way? She couldn't decide, so she put the dungarees aside while she went on with her search.

She came across a sewing kit, finally, and in the same drawer she found two photographs. One was of a girl somewhat younger than herself, who could only have been Don's sister. She looked pretty and plain at the same time, and her smile was open and ingenuous. A few lines at the bottom of the print identified her as Dorothy.

The other picture was not at all the sort which a girl gives her older brother. The most striking effect was that afforded by a gown cut so far off the shoulders that it was in apparent imminent danger of being off altogether. The mouth was a petulant pout of full glistening lips, and what the smile failed to convey in the way of suggestiveness was amply provided by the sultry, sidelong invitation of the eyes. This picture was inscribed, *"To the strong, silent one, from his naughty little Ivy."*

"And I'll bet you really can cling," Betty said to the sly, wise face. She dusted her fingertips together as she droppped the photo back in the drawer.

Without consciously having come to any decision about it, she found herself, a bit later, measuring and fitting herself for a pair of shorts.

The afternoon passed quietly, in the sleepy way of hot after-noons in the woods, and Betty working at the table outside, grew absorbed enough in her sewing to forget the problems which awaited her back in town. She hummed over her work, pulled out stitches and pinned and restitched, and the hours went by unnoticed. Trying on and reworking first the shorts, then her shirt, then her regular dungarees, she was at last stitching busily away in nothing but her own rather unwoodsy panties. Sunlight filtered down in dancing patches through the leaves, covering her naked skin with a lacey, ever-changing pattern as she sat, bare legs crossed in tailor fashion, and bent over her task. Occasionally she straightened and stretched, her rounded breasts rising sharply as she drew a deep breath of the pine-smelling breeze which playing inquisitively through her hair, a picture of young, unspoiled womanhood, brimming with health and still-leashed energies.

A great crashing through the underbrush, coupled with a roaring sailors' chanty, heralded Don's return.

"Hey you!" she cried out. "Just a minute!"

She wriggled into the shorts and shirt in the few seconds before he appeared.

"Something wrong?" he asked innocently.

Too innocently, Betty thought. Don didn't go slamming through the woods like that. He was being discreet, in a rather elephantine way. Blushing, she wondered how long he had been observing her before making his presence known.

She noticed that his fishing creel was heavy, and used that to turn his attention.

"You met the enemy bravely, I suppose?"

"I was fearless," he admitted modestly.

"Show me the old lunker you've been feuding with," she said. "That real wise old granddaddy of them all."

"I put him back to grow wiser. He's too old and stringy to make very good eating."

"You expect me to believe that?"

"It is my turn," said Don, "not to give much of a damn whether or not I'm believed." He grunted approvingly at the shorts.

"Fine for around camp," he said. "But stay out of the brush with them. Turn around. Hmm."

"They don't quite fit," Betty explained. "There wasn't enough material to let out in — some places."

"So I see But then it's always seemed to me that girls' shorts were considered progressively more successful as they made the wearer look more spankable."

"I had no such intention," Betty said shortly, and gathered her sewing as Don slipped off his shirt to wash up. At the door of the trailer she turned. Don was snorting furiously in a splashing shower of suds. For a moment she watched the movements of his sleekly muscled torso, the naked play of the rippling knots in his broad back, the drip of water from the light mat of hair on his heavy chest.

Under other circumstances, she mused, Don Hammond could have been a very attractive person to meet.

CHAPTER NINE
POUR LE SPORT

AFTER supper that evening, Don took Betty for a short hike along one of the trails. Climbing upward to a great shelf of rock, they watched the sun set in a spectacular pageant of unbelievable beauty. A heavy nostalgia crept, sadly-sweet, through Betty's mind. She began to feel homesick, until she wondered what in the world she was homesick for. The tinseled fraud of the Deep Sea Club? If she were to be completely honest with herself, she must admit that, at that moment, there was no place where she would rather be than right where she was, watching the sky burst into glorious, flaming shards of color which slowly swept across the horizon.

"Warm again tomorrow," was Don's reaction.

"And is that all you see in it?" Betty breathed. "All this is just a weather report?"

"See here, young lady," Don said, "you're old enough to realize that some people express their appreciation of things in something less than full capitals. If I don't gush over it, if I don't make like Shelley — well, why the devil do you think I brought you here, instead of puttering around camp?"

"My error," said Betty.

"That's a water hole below us," Don went on. "If we're patient and quiet, we may see something very nice."

And they did, for a short time later a doe with two speckled fawns crept out of the wood and quietly drank. The fawns wanted to play, but the older deer was uneasy. She kept testing the air, and cupped her large ears searchingly toward the ledge.

"She suspects that we're about," Don whispered. "The wind is wrong, so she can't be sure, but they won't stay long."

And, soon afterward, the trio disappeared as quietly as they had come.

"They're so lovely," Betty said as she and Don stood up to go. "I don't see how people can call it sport to shoot them. How many have *you* killed?" she demanded accusingly.

"I can see," said Don, "that you could become quite a nuisance to have around. I am not a professional murderer. I leave that to the world's politicians, who have been doing a much more effective job."

"And aren't you helping them a little bit?" Betty asked. "I seem to have read that you do things with atoms."

"The things which have been learned about atoms," Don told her firmly, "are inherently no more socially destructive than the discovery of any other natural law. Start with the wheel or the inclined plane or where you will — there's nothing which a backward social science hasn't misused. And we don't choose to go barefoot simply because armies march in shoes. With some little knowledge of nuclear fission, destructively-minded men have succeeded in constructing a tremendously frightful threat to a sensible, peaceful future. But that is only one phase of the atom's potential, and where my work touches on bombs at all, it has more to do with the possibility of stripping them of their power, interfering with the reaction so that they fizzle out like squibs. And I came up here to forget about it for a while. So, with your permission, the only explosions we will consider tonight will be those contained in a double handful of popcorn."

Under a hissing gasoline lamp Betty lolled on the couch, dividing her attention between the book she was reading, a bowl of popcorn, and the occupation with which Don was busying himself. Working at a tiny vise, he was leisurely manufacturing a succession of rather large-bodied trout flies.

"How many hundreds of those things does a man need to go fishing?" Betty finally asked.

"This is just something to keep my hands busy while my brain decays," Don grinned. "To — " He looked at Betty's long, bare legs as she stretched. " . . to . . well, to keep my hands busy. These are wet flies, which, I proudly tell myself, are excellent imitations of newly hatched nymphs. Want to try your hand?"

Betty put her book aside and watched the details of the operation. Then she selected her materials from the supply at hand, and went to work.

"Hey, you," Don protested, "these things are supposed to look like something a trout might normally come across. There isn't anything in nature which looks like that thing."

"I like the colors," Betty said, and went on winding thread about the hook.

Finished, the creation was bulky and lop-sided. Its color was mainly a brilliant gold, flecked with spots of green and a double splash of crimson. Don examined it dubiously.

"What is it?"

"A nymph, of course."

"A golden nymph." He matched the color against her hair, and turned her head to the light. "Very attractive."

"Unbelieveable," Betty disparaged. "No one could be fooled by such an obvious fraud."

"I suspect," said Don, ruffling through the feathers, "that there is a hook hidden somewhere in here, in all this fluffy innocence."

"Barbless, Mr. Hammond. One must be sporting about these things."

"Ouch! But sharp. It bites."

"An admonition against over-familiarity, Mr. Hammond."

"The point is well taken, Miss Brooks," Don smiled, handing the fly back. He yawned then, and said, "Mr. Hammond retires early in camp. Do you mind?"

"Of course not. But where ... "

"I am rather long, and the couch is the only thing which accommodates me. The chair behind you opens into a bed which is about your size."

"I don't want to appear prudish," she said, "but I am not accustomed to sleeping in such close quarters with strange men. If you have a cot I could take outside — "

"I haven't."

"Well — the car, then. Would that be all right?"

"You won't be comfortable, but you're welcome to try it. If one of us must leave the trailer — and you're equally welcome to stay — it isn't going to be me. I'm sorry, but I can't see myself as a martyr to your peace of mind."

"I understand your feelings perfectly," Betty said. "And I hope you understand mine."

With two blankets, a pillow and a flashlight, she left the trailer and, removing only her shoes, made herself as comfortable as she could on the back seat of the car. For a few minutes she could see the shadow-figure of Don moving about the trailer. Then the cheerily lighted windows became blank holes of darkness.

She had not been asleep — or had she? Perhaps she dozed, briefly, and something more than her own cramped discomfort had waked her. She did not know what it had been, and, instinctively, she lay quiet while she tried to recall it.

And then it came again. A discreet, but heavy, scratching noise coupled with a thick snuffling, came to her ears. Then silence. Betty strained to locate the source of those sounds, while her eyes pierced futilely into the darkness about her. Something seemed to be moving in the vicinity of the fireplace, but she could not be sure that her senses were not tricking her. Aiming the flashlight in that general direction, she switched it on.

Two fiery eyes glared out of a mountainous bulk of dark fur — a bulk which rose until it towered in grotesque, towering caricature of a human form. Betty had an instant's impression of a snarling lip drawn back over gleaming, yellowish fangs, a dripping tongue lolling in a cavernous mouth. Time ticked by while her throat strangled soundlessly —

Then she was screaming, and she found the horn of the car and was punching it with all her might, and the cry that burst from her was a named called over and over:

"Don! *Don!*"

A beam of light suddenly leaped from the trailer door. It played over the car and, blindingly, into her eyes.

"The fireplace!" she cried. "At the fireplace!"

The light cut a path across the clearing, bur it was empty. A headlong crashing through a thicket was the only evidence that anything had been there.

Don was beside the car, the light in one hand and a revolver in the other.

"What in hell is the matter?" he demanded.

"A — ab — a bear," Betty chattered. "Coming after me, and he got — got as far as the fireplace and — "

"Take it easy," Don said. "Cool off. You saw a bear. All right. Did he have a scar, sort of a white streak, across the top of his nose?"

"A streak across his nose?" Betty demanded, outraged. "How should I know? Should I have gotten his license number?"

"In the first place," Don said, "no bear was after you. He was digging in the fireplace because he smelled burnt fish bones, and the worst thing he might have done was upset the stewpot. I asked about the scar because I suspect it was Old Grumpy. This is his back yard, and we're really the intruders, you know. He pays me a call almost every time I stop here, but I don't think we'll see him again. Not after the reception you gave him."

"Good old Grumpy!" Betty snorted. "I suppose I ought to apologize for having offended an old friend of yours!"

"Not really," Don said. "He's pretty dull company. Something like a playfully destructive drunk. But he probably won't bother you again tonight."

"If you think I'm going to stay out here — " Betty said, swinging the car door open and stepping out. Then she saw that Don was naked.

He, too, seemed to realize it for the first time.

"Sorry," he said. "I sleep raw, and you made it sound like an emergency."

Betty handed him a blanket, which he casually slung over one shoulder. Silently she followed him back to the trailer, casting an occasional glance backward into the forbidding black shadows.

Once inside, Don put away the revolver and tossed the blanket on a chair. While Betty pretended to be very busy elsewhere, he crawled into bed and, with a muffled "good night", turned his face to the wall. Somehow Betty got the impression that he was laughing.

She arranged the chair into a bed and then she began to undress. It was a disturbing sensation, stripping oneself naked while a stranger lay only a few feet away.

She cocked one eye at the place where Don was. The sound of his regular breathing reassured her.

A disciple of Freud, she mused, would probably have much to say on the subject of the series of accidents which had found her naked when Don was near.

CHAPTER TEN

TINGLING BLOOD

HAD Betty attempted to keep a journal of those next few days, it must all have been written in red ink, for unforgettable impressions tumbled over one another so rapidly that no day passed without its own special reason for remembrance.

There was, for instance, the day Don grew angry with her. It was not the sort of thing which one would ordinarily look back upon with any pleasure, and yet it gave her a vast insight upon the way his mind worked, and left her, if not happier, at least more understanding of his nature.

Don had gone off fishing, and Betty, with some knowledge of where he would be, had later cut across country to intercept him as he worked up stream, to ask whether or not a certain species of mushroom which she had found in great profusion was edible. While she waited for him to appear she lighted a cigaret, and she was smoking when he waded into sight. His greeting, however, was somewhat less cordial than she expected.

"Put out that cigaret," he called as soon as he caught sight of her.

Since his own pipe was fuming busily, that seemed like a ridiculous demand, and Betty chose to ignore it.

"I said, put out the cigaret," he repeated as he came closer.

Betty blew smoke rings at him.

His jaw tightened. He reeled in his line, knocked out his pipe into the water, and stowed it away.

"If that thing isn't out by the time I make shore," he said, "you'd better start running."

Betty watched him clamber up the bank and lean his rod against a tree. She began to grow uneasy as he dropped his net and creel and started in her direction. Something in his bearing was too determined to be comfortable. She dropped the cigaret as he came nearer, and retreated a few rods down the trail. She watched as he carefully retrieved the butt and tossed it into the water. Then he advanced toward her. She trotted a few steps and stopped.

"What's this about?" she said peevishly. "Why are you allowed to smoke if I'm not?"

"I was smoking a pipe," he said, "in the middle of the stream. You just dropped a lighted cigaret into a bed of dried leaves and brush — and you know better because I've mentioned it before. This time we'll make the lesson stick. A guest's privilege does not extend to the point of allowing him to burn up the woods."

To make it worse, as they back-tracked down the trail they came across a burnt-out patch of pine needles — mute evidence of an earlier-dropped, and carelessly trod upon, cigaret. Betty began to run then, while Don walked swiftly and grimly after her. Somehow, within the next few moments, she took a wrong turn in the path, finding herself in a bramble-lined *cul-de-sac*.

Betty became dignified.

"See here, Mr. Hammond," she protested, "you can't — "

But he could, and he did.

Sitting down on a fallen tree trunk he took her across his knee, and her dignity evaporated in a wildly thrashing and futilely struggling outrage. And the little things of the forest were silent and listened, puzzling over the strange ways of humans, the gasping squeals, the smacking sound of a determined palm on softly padded flesh.

On her feet again, Betty hitched up her trousers and raced breathlessly back to the camp, determined to take the car and head for home. But somehow she kept putting off her departure, and soon it was time to begin supper.

It was quite incidental, of course, that during the evening, while a quiet shower of rain pattered on the metal roof of the trailer, Betty noticed that some three pairs of Don's socks needed repairs and so set about mending them, while the radio told the wonders of a gay nightclub in the city of Chicago.

Along toward the middle of the week a day dawned which to Betty was to become "the day Don saved my life" — although Don laughed at that and insisted that, even if the worst had happened, she would have had ninety-odd chances out of a hundred to survive it.

It all happened when Betty, left to her own devices one morning, decided to have another try at angling. Taking some of Don's extra equipment, she went off, looking for a spot clear enough to accommodate her rather inexpert efforts. Soon she found it — a large pool, wide and deep, and bounded by boulders, giving her plenty of room to swing a line. Here she went to work, fishing in careful imitation of Don.

She had no idea of what lure she should use, so she tried several successively. Cast after cast proved fruitless. Her wrist began to ache, and beads of moisture soon formed on her brow and ran into her eyes. She wiped them away and kept trying.

It *couldn't* be so difficult to catch a fish, she told herself. She was willing to concede that there was more than plain luck involved, yet here she was, doing everything that she had seen Don do, and having not the slightest success.

A gentle tapping seemed to touch her line, but she couldn't be sure. She tapped back with a twitch of her fingers, and suddenly she felt the full, surging yank of a firm strike. And, rather than becoming excited, she was immediately filled with a calculating calm. She set the hook sharply, and tried to remember everything she had been told or had observed about bringing a fish to net.

It took a surprisingly long time, for the fish was large, tired slowly, and, each time that Betty thought she had worked him into position for capture, found some reserve of energy to carry him off like a shot. At last, though, she felt his weight in the net, and she quickly carried him back from the water, as though he might still find some unorthodox means of escape. When she had him unhooked, she was more impressed with his size than she had been when fighting him He was plump and squirmed healthily up to the very instant when Betty administered the *coup de grace*, and she knew he was a fish of which to be proud. Don, she thought, would be approving.

And what, her mind went on, does that mean to me? I must be getting dotty, out here in the woods, if I'm looking for praise like a school child.

The dark water of the pool shimmered an invitation. Now that her fish was safely creeled, Betty became aware of feeling warm and sticky all over. Since she didn't plan to fish any more, she decided on a quick dip, and, almost as soon as the thought came to her, she began to strip.

Piling her clothes neatly, she picked her way to the bank's edge and waded in. Spring-fed and icy, the water's chill was almost more than she had bargained for, but she set her teeth, plunged forward, and after a breathless gasp or two found that she could enjoy it after all.

Puffing and spouting, she played about like a young, wild woods creature, her body flashing swiftly as she dove after some shining pebble, surfaced to float restfully with her hands casually clasped behind her head. On her back, she noisily sputtered the wavelets which broke over her chin, and eyed the length of her nudity to the tips of her wriggling toes. For some reason she was still thinking of Don and her need of his approval.

She wondered what he thought of her now — as against what he had so obviously thought when they first met. She wondered if they would see each other after this week was over, and hoped that they would. Considering her feelings toward him as objectively as she was able, she decided that she was a little bit in love. It was a good feeling and she liked it. Still, she wondered if she would be feeling this way if they had met in a somewhat more usual fashion. The pattern of their acquaintanceship so far had been anything but ordinary.

A warning chatter of her teeth told her that she had spent enough time in the water. She stroked to shore and climbed over the boulders to a sunny spot where she would dry quickly. Running her fingers through her hair to fluff it, she yawned contentedly and waited for nature to take care of the rest. The sun glared dazzlingly off the hot rocks. She leaned back on her elbows and closed her eyes ...

"Don't move."

It was Don's voice, quiet but penetrating, and very commanding. She opened her eyes and found him standing near the mouth of the pool, but on the opposite side. He was staring intently in her direction — so intently that a curious fear was the first emotion Betty felt.

"Hold still for just ten seconds. Don't move a muscle. Don't speak."

Although every impulse protested, that same fear, made stronger by the peculiar urgency of Don's tone, froze her to the spot. She watched him slip the revolver from its holster, then horrified, realized that it was pointing at her. Into her mind flashed the thought that Don was somehow deranged, that he was either playing some fantastic, insane joke or that he really meant to kill her.

"When I fire," Don said, *"roll to your left, and keep rolling."*

Hair prickled on the back of her neck as she realized that the danger was not Don, but something which she could not see.

The revolver coughed deafeningly, and as though her body had been on springs waiting for release, Betty twisted frantically away from the spot where she had been sitting. A maddened, vicious thrashing in the leaves brought her eyes to a thick, copper-banded body which coiled and knotted about itself in convulsive futility. Betty scrambled to her feet and stared at the thing, unmindful of her nakedness.

"Copperhead," Don said at her side. "You were almost curled up together. If you'd moved your elbow six inches — "

"Don," Betty said weakly, "I . . I . . "

The sun was a bright, burning platter which was coming down on her head. The trees were dancing about in an erratic eclipse. Everything was too bright, but it was hard to see because nothing was in focus. Betty stumbled and clutched at Don's shoulder. Then she was held by his arms, her shivering thighs pressed close to his rough clothing as her knees sagged. Her soft breasts lay tightly against his shirt, and, oddly enough, she was aware of the steady, deep thumping of his heart — that and a pleasant smell of woodsmoke and tobacco.

"Hey, you, don't faint." he said. "It's not done this year."

"I — won't," Betty promised. But she couldn't have said, later, whether or not she kept that promise, for in her memory of the incident there was a brief interlude of floating in blackness. And then Don was kissing her and, naked as she was, she clung shamelessly to him and kissed him back.

Somehow reality returned, and the things about them came into proper perspective.

"I'd better get some clothes on," Betty said, pulling away. "Somehow it seems that every time I take off my clothes I turn around and find you."

Don discreetly gave his attention to the snake while she dressed.

"Been fishing, I see," he said as she finished and stood waiting for him.

She opened the creel, and he whistled. Then, suspiciously, he demanded,

"Did you deceive this poor creature with the promise of a fat, juicy angle-worm?"

For reply Betty indicated the gay wisp of color tied to her leader.

"The golden nymph?" Don exclaimed in half-mock amazement. "That *thing?* Well I'll be damned."

Betty and he grinned at each other in the manner of people who have a private joke.

As they turned up the trail to camp, Don laid his hand on Betty's shoulder.

"Now that the excitement is all over and the balloon has gone up," he said, "do you suppose that you would like to be kissed again?"

"Possibly," Betty admitted.

They tried it again, and they both found that it was very good.

CHAPTER ELEVEN

CAPRICE

O N THE next to the last day of their stay in the woods, Betty managed to get lost. It all happened over a pie.

There were berries of all description growing in and near their campsite, and they formed a welcome addition to the camp diet. Having once managed a batch of corn muffins dotted with blueberries, Betty resolved to attempt something more elaborate — a blackberry pie. Bucket in hand, she started out late in the afternoon to forage the neighborhood.

As always happens in such cases, the ripe berries near at hand proved to be skimpy and of inferior quality, although the bushes were loaded with red ones — which, as everyone knows, is the color of a blackberry when it is green. And so Betty cast further afield, at first staying close to trails she knew, but later straying into side paths and animal runs which were unmarked and new to her.

The afternoon passed, the bucket filled slowly, and Betty was vaguely aware of the unhurried gathering of a storm. It was not until the sky had darkened considerably, however, not until she heard the first mutter of thunder, that she was willing to concede that her bucket was full enough for all practical purposes. She turned, then, to head back to camp.

But which way was camp? It was — no, not in that direction. It must be …

Betty noted, with surprised interest, that she did not know which was the shortest way back. She would have to retrace her steps, at least part of the way, until she came to some familiar landmark.

Finding what she took to be the path she had last left, Betty started cheerily along it — until it petered out to nothing in a tangle of dogwood. Somewhat annoyed, she turned back, apparently passed the place where she had last entered the path, and came to a fork. She took the larger — and ended in a mushy area of swamp grass.

Obviously she had to go to higher ground, so she cut back to where the second arm of the path should have been. Except that it wasn't. There was nothing bigger than a rabbit course in that direction. That was when she realized that she was lost.

Once she climbed atop a large rock and called out two or three times, turning from one direction to another. Her voice startled her. It sounded thin and panicky, and she was sure it would not carry more than a short way. She toiled upward.

Darker, and ever darker it grew. Then, suddenly split asunder by forks of lightning, the heavens opened and an all-engulfing downpour began. Within five minutes Betty was as wet as she could get, and at the end of that time she had come up short against the towering granite face of a cliff, where some glacier of the earth's youth had torn away half a mountain.

Then Betty sank down on a dripping log and, because there was nothing else to do, got ready to cry — not from fear, but from the bitter taste of defeat.

The report of a shot, echoing through the night, brought her to her feet. A second, following almost immediately, helped her to locate the direction. It was Don, she knew, and he was searching for her, trying to signal. Cupping her hands to her mouth she shouted his name into the wind as she had never shouted before.

It seemed like hours. Then came another shot, but seemingly further away. She shouted again and waited.

There was no keeping track of time after that. It could have been an hour afterward when Don found her, or it could have been much more. It was long enough for her to shout herself hoarse and to die half a dozen times over as she waited and feared that he had lost track of her. But finally she caught a gleam of light, then heard Don's voice answer her call. A short while later he appeared, wearing a waterproof parka, carrying a packsack, and casually smoking his pipe upside down.

"Dr. Livingston, I presume?" he said as he dropped the pack and stretched.

Betty threw herself into his arms and tightly clung to him.

"Don, Don" she whispered. "I've been so frightened... But somehow I knew, *I knew* you'd come."

Don turned her face — wet, now, with sudden tears that mingled with the rain — to his. His lips touched the tip of her nose the first time, but soon found their mark, and their mouths clung.

"You had me worried, Betty," he said after a long silence. "You really had me worried this time. He felt the spasm of a chill run through her, and he added, "And I'm not through worrying yet."

"Are we — f -far from ca -camp?" Betty shivered.

"Far enough. I wouldn't take a chance on it now anyway. Let's see what we can do about the situation."

He explored the cliff-side until a shallow concavity, not deep enough to be a proper cave, was revealed in the powerful beam of his light. Sheltered by an overhang, the spot afforded relative dryness and protection from the bite of the wind. A fault in the rock made a natural flue for a fire, and in no time Don had a cheery blaze dancing. Then he turned to his pack.

"This first," he said, producing a pint of brandy. "Two *big* slugs for you."

Dutifully Betty downed a heavy draught of the amber liquor. Neat, it had a tendency to get up her nose, and it stung her throat waspishly, but the warmness in her stomach was gratifying.

Kris Kringle never carried a pack more replete with wondrous gifts dun that which Don toted, nor was the Horn of Plenty more bountiful in its largess. First of all there was the strip of tarpaulin which formed a shelter, the heat from the fire reflecting off the face of the cliff and into the one open side. Next there appeared a sleeping bag with a pneumatic mattress, inflated by a tiny gas cartridge. Then foodstuffs began to appear, requiring, most of them, no more than the addition of water, of which there was no lack.

"We have — we have berries for desert," Betty chattered as another spasm seized her. "I was g-going to ma-make a p-p-pie."

"Fine," Don said. "Another time. Right now —" He produced a wooly towel from somewhere. "Take off your clothes."

"Wh - *what?*"

"You heard me, and you heard right. After the time I had finding you, if I lost you to pneumonia I will be very much annoyed. Off with them! You're going to have supper in bed."

Miserably wet and cold though she was, Betty balked. Don looked at her, and while he was looking her teeth again began to rattle.

"I will count three," he said. "You pick the damndest time to become modest."

At the count of two Betty began to undo her shirt. Don tossed the towel onto the sleeping bag and began to poke at the fire. Then he arranged a drying rack of branches near it and received each piece of clothing as Betty removed it.

"Shirt, frayed," he checked. "Shoes, down-at-heel. Dungarees, patched. Wool stockings, need mending. Hey — that's not all."

"Cap," Betty said, tossing it to him, "too big."

"And *that's* not all. Do you give them to me or do I — ?"

"Panties!" Betty shouted. "$2.98 on clearance!"

"O.K. Now get as close to the fire as you can, and dry yourself. Dry. I have objected to damp beds since I was four."

"You object to — you mean there's only one sleeping bag?"

Don sighed. "My dear Betty," he said. "I brought with me what I could reasonably carry on my back. Did you expect me to come dragging a little red wagon?"

Betty stood stock still, digesting this, the towel draped more or less concealingly in front of her.

"Let's talk this thing over — ", she began.

"For Pete's sake," Don exclaimed in exasperation, "give me that towel! While we're arguing you've gone through six stages of 'flu."

He snatched it away and began a brisk, ungentle, and almost impersonal toweling, starting with Betty's back. He rubbed down to her full hips, then went back to her shoulders, fluffed the back of her hair, and worked down each arm in turn.

"Other side," he said shortly.

The towel moved vigorously, and Betty's skin began to glow with a warmth which was not wholly due to the fact that she was blushing.

"Left leg," he said, and Betty dutifully pointed a toe. "Turn around again."

At last, when she was tingling from her ears to her ankles, Don handed the towel back.

"Maybe I missed a few spots," he suggested.

"You — didn't — miss — anything," Betty said, resentment boiling in her tone. "I've never, *never* — "

"Never been so insulted in your life," Don finished cheerfully. "So sue me."

I like him, she told herself. I more than like him, and I'll go on feeling that way even if — even if... But he's always just a little too much ahead of me, too impatient. Just now, for instance — five minutes more and I'd have taken off my clothes and dried myself without being ordered about like a child. If only he didn't *push* so!"

Don moved a flat rock next to the sleeping bag, and with that for a table they attacked their belated meal. For the sake of appearances, Betty displayed an attitude of injured huffiness at first, but soon forgot it as Don ignored it. The first cup of coffee was scalding hot and used as an antidote against chill. The second, cooler, was strongly laced with brandy and dawdled over with a cigarette. Propped on one elbow, Betty explained how she managed to get lost. Don, squatting on his heels, nodded sympathetically and, strangely enough, offered no criticism.

When they had finished, Don lazily set the tin dishes in a spot where the rain would wash them, yawned, puttered with the fire, and sat down with his back against the side of the cliff. By the way he settled himself, Betty understood that he was telling her he expected to spend the night there.

The next move seemed to be up to her. She did a lot of fast thinking in those next few silent moments. She wanted to be sure that she was right, and that she really knew what she was doing.

"Don," she said, her voice a bit husky from the shouting.

"Hmm?"

"Don't be silly. I won't have you misuse yourself this way."

"Perfectly — ouch! Perfectly comfortable."

"You are not and we both know it. Now look — I have never suggested such a thing in my life, but I do wish you would — would —" (Could she say the words?) " — would come and claim your half of this sleeping bag. And if you won't," she threatened, "if you won't, I'll get up and put on my wet clothes and sit up with you."

Don's face could not be seen, for his hand hid it as he rubbed his nose.

"In that case," he said, "I have no choice."

He unwound his long frame from its cramped position and began hanging his outer clothing on the drying rack. Betty turned her back to him and snuggled into a cooler part of the bag. At least she could give him a warm spot to crawl into.

CHAPTER TWELVE

LADY GODIVA

H "ARRUMPH!"

Taut and straight as a stretched string, now, Betty lay pressed as far as she could get toward her side of the downy sack.

'Don cleared his throat again and then said,

"Uh — candy bar or — or something?"

"No thanks," Betty answered. And then, in a voice that betrayed her waning confidence, "Maybe one more drink, if there is one."

"Oh — sure. Plenty. Here. You can turn around."

Betty saw that he was wearing undershorts no briefer than most bathing suits, still had on his heavy shoes.

They bumped cups, and Betty meditated over her liquor. She was a little bit tight already, and she knew it. Knew it and, far from being distressed by it as she had been with Bobby, was enjoying it.

"Nothing like getting lost in the woods to liven up a party," Don said. He wrapped a light blanket over his broad shoulders. "I guess it hasn't seemed like much of a party to you, though — this last week. Not the sort of show Bobby Morgan puts on, is it?"

Betty stared at him, gulped down the brandy at the bottom of her cup, then held out the cup for more.

"No," she said, "it isn't." And to herself she added, "thank heaven."

"Real gay times, hmm?"

"Oh, terribly. A little wild, sometimes, but always gay — so gay!"

"You must know a lot of Bobby Morgan's friends."

"Oh, scads. I can't remember them all, but they're all such fun! Everybody is so gay all the time!"

"Then perhaps you know my sister?"

"Dorothy? Oh, *dear* Dotty — we all call her Dotty, you know. *So* amusing. Let me see...I met Dotty the night I was arrested for playing Lady Godiva with a policeman's horse. He was such a daring — the horse, that is. Or — no, it was the night my strip-tease act was raided. Anyway, one of those nights when we were all in the cutest jail, having our pictures taken and all."

"I don't find your smartness very amusing. All I want to know is —"

"You great big *dope!*" Betty howled. "Can't I ever get it through that thick, multi-million-dollar, over-educated skull of yours that I am *NOT* one of Bobby Morgan's chippies? I've seen him at the Club, I was invited to one of his parties, and I left when I found out what was expected of me. That's all. Once and for all time, try to understand, will you?"

"But you *do* know Dorothy," Don said suspiciously.

"Only through a photo I saw in the trailer. Looks like a nice kid."

"She is a nice kid. Too nice. That's the trouble. She just can't believe that a Bobby Morgan is — what he is. She's young and trusting and — anything can happen to a kid as naive as she is. Anyway, ,I heard she'd been getting mixed up with that gang recently, and — well, I was looking for her when I ran into you."

"Find her?"

"No."

"And it probably wouldn't have meant a thing if you had. Believe me, I *know!* Sure, she probably knows him. After all, how many people are there in your social circumstances? People who spend their time at boating and at the horse shows and things like that? She's bound to run into him sometime."

"She does know him, of course. And so do I. Our families have been distantly acquainted for years. But I don't want her to get involved with any of that bunch of parasites. You know why. You know what they are."

"But I don't see that it's your responsibility. If your family knows — "

Don broke in impatiently. "Dorothy is still young enough to be adolescently rebelling against her parents. Every normal kid goes through that — otherwise we'd never grow up. But it means that anyone of whom they disapprove is going to be defended by her — and she'll become more involved than ever with that person, just to assert her independence. And besides, my father has a terrific temper — some of which he passed on to me, I'm sorry to admit. If he heard a word breathed linking Dot's name to Bobby Morgan, he'd probably set off and wring his neck in public."

"And you want to beat the old boy to it."

Don grinned. "It wouldn't be so undignified for me. I am a well-known playboy. Very gay. Whoopie!"

"More," Betty said, holding out her cup. "Go on talking. I like it."

"You have the most wonderful blue eyes," Don said. "I know they're blue, but in the firelight they look almost black, and — "

"Wrong kind of talk," Betty objected. "Tell me about yourself, what you think about — things like that."

"All right. I *think* you have the most wonderful blue eyes. I *thought,* when I first met you, that you were going to be a terrific problem — and you are, only not in the way I expected. I thought you were going to ruin my week, but I've enjoyed this trip more than any of the others. I — "

"Sure. One day I damn near burn up the woods, and then you have to come hunting me in a storm. Exactly what *is* your idea of fun?"

"Sitting here like this, getting a little bit high with you now that I know you're safe. Talking with you in the trailer, evenings. Watching you as you sit reading at night. Waking up in the dark and listening to your breathing for a few minutes before I go back to sleep. Betty ... "

Although her pounding heart was crying out to him, although she wanted to throw herself into his arms, Betty simply rolled the brandy in the bottom of her cup, breathed its pungency, and let the silence gather about them.

Was Don really what she wanted? Or was it just the result of being thrown so closely together for these last few days? Wouldn't she have felt much the same toward any reasonably attractive young man with whom she had lived alone for almost a week? And what did Don want — really? A hat-check girl from a crooked gambling joint? It was almost time to be leaving the camp, and when they got back to the city, back to the normal, so different lives which awaited them there — what then?

"I though we were going to be sensible about all this," she said.

"How in the devil can a man be sensible when he's in love?" Don asked irritably. "Betty, this thing has been creeping up on me for days, but it finally caught me while I was looking for you tonight. When I saw the glare of your fire signal, I stopped and sat down. I had to. I was shaky all over — from relief. And I couldn't understand it at first. Then it hit me squarely between the eyes. I'm in love with you Betty. As much in love as a man can be."

"Don," Betty said. "I — I .. "

Naked to the waist, she sat upright and put aside what remained of her drink. Don was looking at her, but she did not mind that. She liked it. She stared into his eyes and was glad for what she saw there. Yes, he loved her. Don loved her! Her whole being silently sang it to the world.

"I don't know what to say," she began again. "Except that I'm glad. I'm awfully glad you love me, Don — because I love you so - much."

She half flung herself, then, to meet his quick, tight embrace, gave her lips almost before they were sought, drew herself closer and closer to him, as though to make their anxious bodies one. And now she knew what it was she had waited to find, why she had fought so vehemently against Bobby Morgan's jaded lechery. She wanted to give herself now — wholly, and without reservation or shame. Something which had slept in her seemed to have leaped into vibrant, burning awareness. Her body was consumed by a throbbing, pulsating need; all her senses were centered on the sudden new thing born in her out of the mingling of her heart's love and her body's passion. She squirmed voluptuously, gasping as Don's tender demands found their response in an ever-heightening urgency. And so, in love and trust and happy, willing wonderment, Betty found the consummation of her womanhood, and knew that it was good.

A long time later, briefly awakened from sleep by some forest sound, Betty lay warmly on Don's arm, her golden head resting on his shoulder, and watched the slow swing of the stars in the clearing sky. She was happy as she had not realized it was possible to be happy, and she had a closer sense of oneness with all of the Creator's work than she had ever known. She was Don's woman, with everything she had. Only one small twinge of conscience bothered her. At one point Don had asked,

"Betty — darling — are you — is this the first time for you?"

And the answer, quick and thoughtless as instinct, had been, "No."

A lie. But a white lie. She would explain it to him some day. Explain that wanting him, wanting all of his love so much, she had been afraid that if he thought her a virgin he might not possess her then, might, out of some doubt of their future, withhold the final measure of her happiness. For she needed him, and in the midst of her love, feared for that love.

CHAPTER THIRTEEN

ONE-HANDED KISS

BREAKING up camp was a bleak affair. Don was his usual competent self, but those little chores which fell to Betty were dawdled over and done so half-heartedly that Don could not help notice.

"We'll be back again," he said with an understanding grin.

"I wonder," Betty said, half to herself. "It's funny — I was so angry with you for bringing me up here, and now I'd be happy to sit down and split a bottle of beer with Old Grumpy, the bear."

In time, everything was packed. Don hitched the trailer to the car and got behind the wheel. Betty stood looking out at the little pond for a few minutes and then got in beside him.

As they drew near to Betty's street, Don pulled the trailer into a parking lot and left it.

"To make your home-coming less conspicuous," he said. Dusk was gathering, and he had switched on the lights when the car pulled up at Betty's apartment.

"You'll feel quite at home in my place," Betty assured him as she led the way up the two flights of stairs. "It's just about the same size as the trailer."

She settled him in the most comfortable chair, mixed a fast collins, and seated herself briefly on the arm of the couch, watching him.

"I wish I had time to enjoy playing hostess for a change," she said. "But I want to shower and see what it feels like to get into a dress again."

"And then?"

"I hadn't planned for then."

"What about the Deep Sea Club? You're through there, of course?"

Betty's face sobered.

"Yes, I'm through there. Tomorrow — the want-ads again. I suppose I'll have to stop in there sooner or later. I've got a week's pay coming — two weeks, if I counted the 'vacation' Rocky gave me. And I'll need that money."

"Then let's do that first. I'll go with you. I've always wanted to see how that joint operates."

"I don't think you should. I don't want you getting mixed up in anything messy. And it will be messy, I know. No, there's no reason for you to get entangled in my affairs."

"I'm pretty deeply entangled with you right now," Don pointed out. "I'll go along."

Betty's protests continued even through the bathroom door as she prepared to shower, but the deafening rush of water finally silenced them. She returned, after a while, fresh, crisp, and looking wholly feminine in a dress which was her current favorite.

"I hope you like it," she said to Don.

He liked it. Later, as he wiped the fresh lipstick from his mouth, he said,

"A wise choice. It doesn't muss easily. Wear it often."

They left and drove to the Deep Sea Club.

It was a quiet hour for the Club. A man and a woman who were drinking very little and who were noisily drunk sat at the bar, along with a morose man who was drinking prodigiously and was not at all drunk. Rocky was not in sight, but with Don two paces behind her Betty marched toward an unobtrusive door near which a stocky, thoughtful-faced individual lounged, his attention divided between a racing paper and a toothpick which he took from his mouth occasionally to examine for signs of wear. At their approach the paper was put down on a table and the tooth-pick laid carefully beside it for future reference.

"I want to see Rocky," Betty said.

Eyes without expression flickered from Betty and traveled slowly over Don.

"He might want to see you," the flat voice said to Betty, "but I ain't so sure about this guy. Wait here."

A wall button was touched. There was a pause, then the latch buzzed and the hood disappeared behind the door. Betty said quietly,

"Rocky is probably giving us the once-over right now, through the Judas hole in the door. Don — that gangster is armed. Rocky too, probably. If there's any argument — even the slightest — please, *please don't* start anything. It isn't worth it."

"I came carrying a pea-shooter myself," Don informed her.

"Don! You shouldn't have! These men aren't normal people. They're twisted and vicious, and they'd as soon shoot you in the back as — "

"Then I won't turn my back. Here comes our friend again."

The door swung open, and the thoughtful man jerked his head in a chilly invitation. Betty entered first, and as Don followed he crowded to one side to avoid the quick, jostling effort of the thoughtful one to bump his shoulder. The light tap of fingers at his hip and jacket pockets he ignored as though he had not noticed them.

Rocky was standing behind the paper-strewn desk with his arms outspread, fingertips lightly resting on the glass top. He was smiling.

"Well," he said. "So you've come back."

The door clicked behind them. The thoughtful man made shuffling noises in a corner and then became very quiet.

"Just long enough to pick up my pay," Betty said. "I don't think I'm cut out for your job, Rocky."

"I figured on something like that when I heard about how you left Morgan's party. You ain't introduced me to your new friend, kid."

"It isn't necessary," Betty said.

"No, it ain't. I recognized him right away."

"I just came to be paid off, Rocky."

"Paid off..." Rocky appeared to muse over this. "Yeah, you sure got somethin' comin' to you. Plenty, in fact. I'm surprised you come back to collect it. Only your friend here makes it a little awkward."

Rocky took the stub of a cigar and lighted it, blew at the end until it glowed brightly. Then he addressed himself to Don.

"Look, pal," he said, "maybe you don't know exactly what you stepped into. I don't know how you come to know our little friend here, or what sort of bait she put out to get you to come here. But it was all a mistake, see? Best thing I can think of for you to do is turn around and go home."

"Thanks. I'll stay a while," Don said.

Rocky sighted through a smoke ring which he aimed at the ceiling. "I always hate to see a man make a mistake," he observed. "Now I know you ain't looking for any trouble. Neither am I. But I got some private business with this — this friend of yours, and I'd like to get it over with without any complications. Let me tell you something. She ain't anybody you ought to know in the first place, see? You maybe listened to some sob story and you got all tied up in it. But this is something that don't concern you. It's like a business matter, see? I put somebody out on a job and then I get the old double X on it. I don't like that. It ain't businesslike."

"Don," Betty said in a low voice, "let's get out of here."

"Not just yet," Don said. "I'm getting interested in this."

"Mister," Rocky said, his voice beginning to get ragged with irritation, though the smile still remained, "what goes on in the private life of one of these chippies just ain't part of your show.

You can find dozens more the same way you found this one. Se blow. Take off, and go back to a neighborhood where you know your way around. I got business with this little dame and I don't need any witnesses, even if you wanted to watch, which I don't think you do."

"Miss Brooks and I," said Don in a voice which seemed to purr, "will leave when you have paid her two weeks salary."

"I guess you leave now," said the flat voice from the corner.

Don shoved the revolver away and stepped toward the thoughtful man.

"That's a pretty big gun for a little man," he said. "Know how to use it?"

"Yeah. First you slip the safety catch, like this ... "

The click was loud and final. Don said,

"I guess I'll be going."

Keeping his eye on the automatic, he turned to the door, stumbled against a chair, and went down on one knee. The thoughtful man started to grin, then stopped as something flashed in Don's hand. Things began to happen.

Fire spat from a spot near Don's waist, and over the roaring chug of the thirty-eight came the brief, high-pitched sound of a slug striking off steel. The thoughtful man blinked and looked at his hand as his numbed fingers let the automatic drop with a thud. Don waved the revolver meaningly in Rocky's direction. Rocky laid his hands flat on the desk.

"I don't carry a rod," he said quickly. "I don't ever carry a rod." Don shoved the revolver away and stepped toward the thoughtful man. Shards of lead had pulped the palm of the man's hand, and the fist that drove at Don's head was bloody, but it had purpose. Don threw two hard blows into the man's face as he slipped under the hooking right, paused to kick the forty-five out of reach, and was almost caught as a chair was swung toward his jaw. Rocky started around the desk just in time to catch the full force of the chair across the throat as Don flung it like a baseball bat. He went back behind the desk and sat down, holding his neck.

"Don!" Betty cried. "Don, stop it! Don't!" And, even as she called to him, she knew that there would be no stopping Don now until his unleashed rage was spent.

The thoughtful man had grown up in a world where no niceties of combat were expected or known. He kicked and gouged and would have used his teeth if the opportunity had offered, and Don answered each dirty tactic with one more vicious. A bloody slime began to drip from the thug's nose, and then from his ears, and still Don's balled fists drove without mercy into the mushing face, across the often-broken nose. The man fell to his knees, and Don lifted him and hit him again.

"Please, please Don!" Betty almost sobbed. "You'll kill him if you don't stop!"

Don looked at her with narrowed, bloodshot eyes as he knocked the man into a corner. There was little of recognition in those eyes now, but he let her catch his arm and hold it tightly pressed in both her hands. Then a mist seemed to clear, and he was really looking at her again. He strode to the desk.

"Pay the lady," he said to Rocky. "Don't bother to figure the tax just now." A bell buzzer began to sound, and there were voices outside the door. "And call off your hounds," Don added.

Rocky had trouble with his voice, but he finally managed it.

"It's all right," he called. "Just a friendly argument. Go on back."

He fished a handful of bills from his wallet and laid them on the desk. Don swooped them up and handed them to Betty.

"Count this," he said. "We don't want to make another trip."

"It's enough," Betty said without looking. "Don, please let's go now."

"Sure," he said.

CHAPTER FOURTEEN

PROPOSITION

DON leaned his head back in the chair and sighed with the exaggerated patience of an impatient man while he allowed Betty to rub an ice cube over a puffy mouse under his left eye.

"It won't do you the least bit of good to make those noises," she said. "Sit still."

"Want to go out somewhere tonight, now that you're back with all the bright lights and citified ways?"

"I do not. I want to stay home and get myself ready to look for another job tomorrow. We'll eat here, if you'll go to the store.

"I'll go to the store, but I strongly disapprove of the rest of the program. What's wrong with working at my place?"

"Your place?"

"Sure. The lab office. Secretarial stuff. Girl Friday, as the want-ads say. Can you keep records, accept shipments, write a nagging letter, smile at the right people, keep the lunatic fringe out of our hair?"

"It sounds simple, the way you say it. But let's be honest. You're just making up a job for me, aren't you?"

"Honestly, no. We've needed someone around there for a long time. There are seven people in that office, and not one of them is really the right person to take charge of things."

"No." Betty shook her head. "If you can't find a straw-boss out of the bunch you have working there, a stranger who knows nothing about the work isn't going to help. I wouldn't want to try it, Don."

"O.K., then," he said, "Here's another job. Pretty much the same thing, working for my mother. Her present secretary is leaving next week. Of course I'll have to warn her that I'll keep trying to steal you for the lab — "

"Your mother has a secretary?"

"One of the penalties of trying to do some good with your money instead of keeping it all to yourself," Don grinned. "Half a dozen foundations to administer, a children's camp, a museum of art, an institute of documentary films, a society for social research, a program for wild-life conservation — oh, she manages to keep herself quite busy, as well as in hot water most of the time. You ought to see the mail there is to plough through. She's on every sucker list in the country, and most of them abroad. And then there are the individual appeals for aid in one form or another — heart breakers, some of them. She tries to see that all that stuff is screened, to separate the phonies from the cases that really need attention, and then do something about them."

"She sounds wonderful," Betty said.

"You'll like her. You'll meet her anyway, soon, but I really think you'd fit in with what she's trying to do. She'll work you like a dog when she thinks you're up to it, but never as hard as she works herself. And then, suddenly, when you think you're at the breaking point, she'll turn around and do something that shows she's been reading your mind, almost. Something so nice and human that — well, that you want to ask her if you couldn't start work an hour earlier from then on."

"Horrors!" Betty laughed.

"She believes in what she's doing, you see. And she'll make you believe in it, too. There's a lot of responsibility involved in the job, because it has to do with real people and real problems. What do you say?"

"I'll take it," Betty answered promptly. "That is, if you're sure there really is such a job."

"I'll call her now," Don said, reaching for the phone. "We'll run out and get the formalities over with tomorrow. Oh — one thing more. She'll ask if I'm going to drive out and spend the evening in the bosom of the family, spend the night there. What do I say?"

Betty looked at the bed, now disguised as a couch. Don followed her eyes.

"I have heard," he offered, "that if they're big enough for one, they're big enough for two."

"Tell her," said Betty, "that you're sorry, but you can't make it."

"Who's sorry?" Don asked.

"I'll make out a grocery list," said Betty. "And don't forget to stop at the drug store."

CHAPTER FIFTEEN
ATOMIC DUST

WITHIN a week Betty was completely at home in the household of the senior Hammonds. Had her confidence in Don been less, she might have hesitated to enter such an ambiguous situation — secretary to the mother of the man with whom she was carrying on an intense love affair — but Don had been very persuasive in assuring her that there need be no complications.

"You will find that my mother asks very few personal questions," he told her. "She understands, of course, that I have some sort of very special interest in you, but she'll be content to wait to find out what it is. My father — well, he likes to believe that he has a nineteenth-century Continental attitude toward the relation of the sexes. He'll probably chase you himself, in a heavily gallant way, until he's satisfied that you're interested in me only. By which time mother, being no dope, will have brought up her heavy guns and so deeply engaged him in a flirtation with herself — "

The arrangement of meals was informal and flexible. Since the elder Hammonds breakfasted together, Betty usually took that meal with Don's sister Dorothy.

With Dorothy she made friends slowly. It was not that the girl meant to be unfriendly — Betty knew that. It was simply that she was still, as Don had said, an adolescent. In rebellion against the restrictions of childhood, she was suspicious also of everyone connected with her parents, and the fact that Betty was only a few years her senior was not enough to keep her from maintaining an alert withdrawal.

There was no unpleasantness in the girl's attitude. Rather, she seemed simply indifferent. She spoke cordially enough, and managed enough polite courtesies to indicate that she did not actively dislike Betty, but at the same time she offered no opening in her own shell of reserve.

And Betty liked her. She wanted to be friends with Don's sister. Her own nature was such that she wanted to give a little of her love to everyone close to Don. And, more than that, as she studied the girl day after day, Betty became convinced that she was not as happy as she might be. Though there were moments when the girl appeared to be bubbling inside with her own joy in living, there were also times when something somber and depressing seemed to have clutched her mind. Her own period of growing into an adult world was not so far behind that Betty had forgotten some of the wrenching miseries of that age, and, though she tended now to remember them with a bit of wry amusement, she knew that there were very real problems which a little sympathetic understanding could do much to erase. Patiently, Betty campaigned against Dorothy's coolness, and bit by bit began to gain some measure of her confidence.

She was able to give more time to Dorothy than would have been the case had she been able to see Don as often as she wished. After the first several days of her new employment, Don twice called to cancel dates which they had arranged.

"We're tied up with something pretty big down at the lab, puss," he explained. "For the next two months things are going to be pretty hectic. Odd hours, long sessions — I'm afraid I won't be able to make any very definite appointments. You understand, don't you?"

"Of course," Betty replied. "Don, I don't want you ever to feel that you can't give everything your work demands because of me. We have lots of time ahead of us."

"A lifetime," Don promised. "Well, then, we'll call off next Saturday and — suppose I give you a ring sometime next week?"

And that was the way things went. What little time Don had free never seemed to coincide with Betty's schedule. She missed him, she was lonely at times, and yet she was happy to be able to feel that she was not a weight about his neck, that he was free to do what he must do without the pressure of any demands from her.

CHAPTER SIXTEEN
BLOSSOMING PROMISE

ONE early afternoon as Betty was about to leave the house, Dorothy came skipping down the stairs carrying a beach bag.

"Hi," the younger girl greeted. "Going into town?"

"Just to do some mailing. Registered things that should go out today."

"Get your swimsuit, Betty," Dorothy said.

"There's the film budget to go over." Betty half-heartedly objected.

"Nonsense," said Mrs. Hammond firmly. "Nothing I can't do myself. I'll be completely out of touch if I allow you to take everything on your shoulders. Out of here now, both of you."

A few minutes afterward the two girls swept past the swimming pool and down the winding drive in Dorothy's Jaguar two-seater.

"The pool's nice," Dorothy observed as she turned onto the open road and opened the throttle, "but I like the ocean. More room — and I like lots of room."

After a pause in town for Betty to take care of her letters they sped on singing tires toward the Sound.

The Hammond's beach cabana was an unpretentious, gay little thing, far more in keeping with its purpose than many of its more showy neighbors. It was intended for fun, and made no effort to impress. With its striped awnings let down and a few pieces of brightly painted beach furniture moved out onto the terrace, it came to life a few moments after the girls' arrival.

"Not many people on the beach this afternoon," Dorothy mentioned. "I like that." She gestured toward a white-painted flag pole with a tilt of her curly head: "Shall we fly the Jolly Roger?"

"I don't know. Are we pirates today?"

"We usually hoist the old boy as a signal to our friends that visitors are welcome. Oh, let's skip it. I don't feel very social."

She led the way to the dressing room where they were to change. Betty, slipping out of her own dress, casually watched as Dorothy undid her blouse and wriggled out of a rather tight skirt. The girl, slim and compact in her ridiculously inadequate dance-set, eyed Betty somewhat less casually, and with an obvious, frank interest.

"I wish I looked like you," she said as Betty, completely naked, reached for her two-piece suit. "Luscious."

Betty paused. She had never thought of her body with that term in mind. She turned to a mirror and looked at herself.

"Nonsense," she said, unconsciously using one of Mrs. Hammond's habitual responses.

"It's not nonsense," Dorothy insisted. "Here, look at us together."

Rapidly she put aside the last stitch of her clothing and came to stand beside Betty. The mirrored nude figures were studies in contrasts — one dark and girlish in its blossoming promise, the other a sparkling blondeness, more definite in its moulded maturity.

"I haven't a *bad* shape," Dorothy observed critically. "In fact it's sort of cute. But next to you I look like a spindly legged calf."

"I don't see a thing wrong with your shape," Betty protested. "You haven't stopped growing yet. If you had a bit more of — of anything — it would be too much."

"Our waists are almost the same," Dorothy mused, "but look at what's above them. My ribs stick out. And my hips — I'm actually bony. I think I'll wail."

Betty studied herself more carefully. She was sure that she had not added a fraction of an inch to the places where a girl should be slender. And yet, in the places where a woman should be rounded and plump — in those places it did seem that her femininity was expressing itself more definitely. There was a hint of softness here and there. Not lusciousness, she decided. Dot had been too enthusiastic. But she was becoming more womanly. She decided that she liked it.

Suddenly she caught sight of her own preoccupied face, serious and thoughtful in its study, and she burst into laughter.

"What a pair of sillies we are!" she exclaimed. "Last one in the water is an old maid — or worse, if there is anything worse."

Later, as they lay on the sand near the water's edge and basked in the hot, brassy beat of the sun, Dorothy said abruptly,

"You know, Bet — I like you."

"I'm glad of that," Betty replied. "I wasn't sure."

"I wasn't sure either when I first met you. I was afraid you'd try to be all palsie-walsie, like mother's last secretary. She seemed to think that part of her job was to keep tabs on me. She was forever pumping away, wondering where I'd been and where I was going — and then always managed to mention things to mother, in a way that made it seem that I was sneaking about. Just because I don't choose to tell my family, or anyone else, everything I do."

"Hmm," Betty observed noncommittally.

"Heavens," Dorothy went on, "I'm not a child any longer. And I don't go around asking my parents what *they've* been up to lately. I don't criticize *their* friends. I don't suggest that they go to bed or get up at a certain hour. All I'm asking is to be left alone."

"Of course it's natural for your parents to worry about such things," Betty pointed out gently. "They've been doing it all the years of your childhood, and I suppose it gets to be a habit."

"Oh I know. And they're dears, really — both of them. But they can't believe that I'm not still their little girl in pigtails."

"They will. You'll just have to give them time."

Dorothy pushed out her under lip and looked wise.

"Maybe they'll have to — sooner than they expect," she said mysteriously.

This remark was so obviously designed to arouse curiosity that Betty chose not to be curious. She hummed softly to herself, and after a few expectant moments Dorothy said,

"You simply don't pry, do you?"

"I try not to. Disappointed?"

"Yes, darn it! Here I've gone ahead and almost decided to tell you all about my great big secret, and you just aren't interested!"

"Everybody loves secrets. That's why they get around so fast." Betty lazily turned to toast herself on the other side.

"I don't think any secret would get around very fast if *you* were keeping it," the younger girl said. "I don't know anything about you, why Don introduced you to mother, or — "

"Prying, Dot?"

"O.K., *O.K.*," Dorothy laughed. "Well, here's my big secret. I'm engaged to be married."

Silence. Then, from Dorothy, a petulant, "Well?"

"Well? Oh — that's nice."

Is that all? Don't you think it's exciting?"

"Not very. It's not my engagement."

"But I'm just a *child!*" Dorothy wailed. "In pigtails, almost! So of course we don't dare tell our families. You can see why we have to be discreet. He scarcely ever comes to the house, unless he's with a party. You'd never guess who it is — and it's someone you know, too."

"I hope you'll be very happy," Betty said.

Dorothy beat the sand in mock desperation.

"You're supposed to *guess*," she protested.

"Oh. The delivery boy. No, he comes alone. The caterer's assistant with the long hair? No — I guess he wouldn't do ... I know — little Freddie from next door. He's always part of a gang on bicycles. I knew he had a crush on you, but I didn't know it was that serious."

"It's Oliver Marks," Dorothy said triumphantly.

"Ah ha!" Betty exclaimed.

"End of secret," Dorothy finished.

"Swim?" Betty suggested to Dorothy.

They splashed out into the water again, and were standing waist-deep in the pulsing lift of the swell when Dorothy suddenly grasped Betty's arm.

"Wait," she said quickly.

Betty followed her gaze and saw a group of half a dozen people in bathing togs coming rather boisterously down the beach.

"Let's swim out behind those rocks," Dorothy said in a whisper, although her normal voice would not have carried to the party.

The two girls churned their way quietly to a point where there was little likelihood of being seen, and from there they watched while the group went up to the cabana.

Treading water, Betty turned to watch the figures as they cut across a low dune.

"I guess we'd better go back," Dorothy was saying. "I've had enough of this for one day."

Her voice was that of a small girl frightened in the dark.

"Yes," Betty said. "We'll go."

She too had recognized Bobby Morgan.

CHAPTER SEVENTEEN
BROWN LEGS

W HATEVER Dorothy's problem might be, Betty was grimly sure of one thing. If Bobby Morgan was involved in it, the matter was quite likely to be ugly.

Whatever Dorothy's problem might be, Betty was grimly sure of one thing. If Bobby Morgan was involved in it, the matter was quite likely to be ugly.

The buzzer on the extension phone sounded. It was Don, and he sounded tired and a bit depressed.

"I'd hoped I could see you this evening," he said, "but it doesn't look as though I can make it. We're up to our ears down here. Next thing they'll be moving cots in so we won't have to leave even to sleep."

"Does this happen often?" Betty asked. "I'm not complaining. I just like to know what to expect."

"Only twice in the last year. One of the men gets onto something that looks real hot and we're off in a cloud of atomic dust. Generally it fizzles out. But there's always a chance that this time may be different."

"You sound awfully beat up."

"You don't sound so gay yourself. Anything wrong?"

"Nothing that a few squirts of Flit wouldn't cure," Betty replied. "No — I'm all right, Don."

"Well, take care of yourself. How's the campaign with Dot coming along?"

"We're going to be friends."

"Good. She needs a friend. She needs *you* for a friend."

"Me?"

"Sure you. You're man's best friend. Woman's too."

"Oh, now we're just friends. And I thought all along you were going to get me into the movies."

"Did I promise you that? Well, I will, I will. If you mention my name and give the cashier eighty-five cents you can get into the Bijou any night except Saturday."

With the conversation switched safely away from Dorothy, they continued to talk for several minutes. Betty was always amazed later to find out how much time they had spent on the wire. It never seemed long.

Several days later a short conversation with Dorothy strengthened her conviction that Bobby Morgan was a decided factor in the girl's periods of withdrawal and depression. The scene was the garden, where Betty was picking a bouquet for her room. A shadow fell across the flower bed, and, recognizing it, she said without turning,

"Good morning, Dot."

"You'd make a great detective," the girl said, seating herself on a stone bench and swinging her bare, brown legs. "Or maybe you are already."

"I'm afraid not. Just a poor woikin' goil."

Dorothy plucked at a loose thread on her shorts and said,

"I've been trying and trying to remember where I've seen you before you came here, and I think I've got it. The Deep Sea Club?"

"Could be," Betty said, sniffing a yellow rose.

"I've been there a couple of times. I guess you wouldn't have noticed me."

"Lots of people stop in there."

"I'm sure of it now. You were at the check room."

"You get a cigar."

"I don't want you to think — but maybe you'd rather not talk about it."

"I don't mind. Is checking hats something one shouldn't want to talk about?"

"I suppose it's just one more way of making a living. Tell me, is it true that the gambling is fixed? You know, crooked?"

"I never had anything to do with that part of the place. I suppose I've heard the same rumors you have."

"It seems funny," Dorothy said. "A person like you working in a joint like that."

"We can't always have things the way we'd like them."

"I hope you won't mention anything about me being there," Dorothy said, apparently anxious as a sudden thought occurred to her. "Golly, I let the cat out of the bag, didn't I?"

"I never saw you there," Betty reminded her. "Anyway, I don't think the subject is likely to come up."

"I suppose not. But just the same, I shouldn't have let that pop out. Mother would have kittens if she knew, and Dad would flip his wig."

Betty stood trimming the stems ends of her flowers, and Dorothy finally said, with forced casualness,

"Do you know Bobby Morgan?"

At last the name was out! Betty became very busy with the gardening shears.

"We've met."

"What do you think of him?"

"Not much."

Dorothy's leg stopped swinging.

"Have you — have you ever been out with him?"

Betty turned and faced the girl.

"Don't you think I've answered enough questions for a while? When does it get to be your turn?"

Biting her lip, Dorothy said, "I'm sorry. I didn't mean to offend you. I'm just naturally curious as a cat."

"And so am I. So you'll know *I* don't mean any offense either when I ask why you hid from Morgan at the beach the other day."

Dotty jumped up, her face white and strained.

"I don't know what you mean!" she exclaimed. "I was — it was one of the girls I was avoiding! She — we had a quarrel about something."

"Then what are you getting excited about?" Betty asked quietly.

"I — I don't know what you mean," Dorothy repeated, flustered. "I've got to get back to the house. I just remembered something — an appointment."

"When you're ready to talk about it, let me know, Dot," Betty said.

She turned back to the flowers. Without further words, Dorothy started across the lawn to the house. Halfway there she broke into a run and Betty sensed that she was crying.

CHAPTER EIGHTEEN
DOLL BABIES

I T all happened at once. There was no rumbling warning of impending disaster, no slow march of events to prepare her for the blow when it fell. Suddenly the sky fell down and the sun was blotted out. It was as simple as that.

Betty was studying financial statements in the library one morning when the butler came to the door to announce that a Miss Dorset was calling. Supposing that it was some business matter, Betty stepped into the main hall to greet the visitor.

"Mrs. Hammond is not at home," she explained immediately. "I'm her secretary. Can I be of any assistance?"

Before the other replied, Betty realized that this was a face which she had seen before. It was — yes, it was the "Ivy" in the picture she had found in Don's trailer.

"I know my way around, thank you," said the caller in a tone that was a bit impatient, a very little bit annoyed.

"I'm afraid I don't quite understand," Betty said. "Mrs. Hammond didn't mention that she expected a call, Miss — Miss Dorset."

The other's slightly feline eyes stared.

"My dear young lady," she informed Betty, "you are obviously quite new at your job or you would understand that I am not in the habit of making a formal appointment to call at this house. Smithers!" She called to the butler who was hovering near by.

"Yes, Miss Dorset?"

"The usual. Not too much vermouth. I'll be in the library."

She swept past Betty without another word. Open-mouthed, Betty turned to the butler.

"Say, Smitty, what's going on here? Is she part of the family?"

"Oh, no, Miss Brooks. Not yet. That is — no. But she's a very close friend of young Mr. Hammond. She's been in Europe until this last week, I understand."

Betty went back to the library. The comfortable leather chair in which she had been working was now occupied by Ivy Dorset, and the papers which she had left on its seat had been carelessly pushed to the floor. Saying nothing, Betty picked them up and carried them to the desk. Ivy, who had been roughly flipping through the pages of a handsome edition of Boccaccio's *Decameron,* apparently looking for illustrations, turned the book face down and gazed idly out of the window.

Smithers arrived with the cocktail tray. A martini, Betty noted. Ten-thirty in the morning seemed like an early start on martinis. She tried to concentrate on the report she was reading. In the room there was a clock whose ticking she had never noticed. She noticed it now. It bothered her.

"Damn!"

Ivy had spilled part of her drink over the tooled morocco of *The Decameron.* Her concern, however, seemed to be mainly directed toward a spot on her suit cuff. She scrubbed at it with a napkin and then wiped her fingers. She did not wipe the book.

"Oh, Miss — I don't know your name … "

"Brooks." Betty wondered if Ivy Dorset heard it even then.

"Yes. Will you go out to my car and take Fuji for a bit of a run? The poor little beastie must be going simply wild by now."

After the first shock of amazement, Betty didn't know whether she was going to laugh aloud or explode with sarcastic indignation. She managed to do neither.

"I'm afraid I'm rather busy just now," she said levelly.

A tiny gasp was the effect of this refusal.

"I *must* say! You *are* an employee of this household, are you not?"

"Mrs. Hammond employs me to take care of such matters as those on which I am now working," Betty affirmed.

"And permits you, I take it, to carry out or reject an order as it suits your convenience?"

Betty's pulse began to jump angrily.

"My duties are fairly familiar to me. I am sure that Mrs. Hammond would not care to have them neglected for the purpose of attending to the natural functions of little beasties. Further than that, I might point out that I am responsible, to some degree, for the proper care of Mrs. Hammond's papers and the contents of this library."

With that she pushed back her chair, stepped across the room, and slipped the mistreated book from beneath Ivy's drumming fingers. Straightening the bent page, she snapped the volume shut, wiped the cover with Ivy's napkin, and returned the book to its place in the shelves.

"Your insolence apparently knows no stopping point," Ivy Dorset said, her catlike eyes poisonous. "I shall make it a point to see that Mrs. Hammond makes clear to you your position in this household — and mine."

"I'm sure you will," Betty agreed. "And now, if you'll excuse me, I'll get on with my work."

The other woman had already touched a bell-pull, summoning Smithers. His response was so prompt that Betty was sure he had been standing just outside the door.

"Bring me another martini," Ivy Dorset said sharply. "In the music room."

Smithers stood aside as she hurried out of the room. Grave and correct, the butler followed. At the door he turned, still solemn, and abruptly flashed an approving wink at Betty.

Betty's blood pressure was almost down to normal when, some half hour later, she heard Ivy's car digging up the gravel as it roared out of the drive.

As soon as Mrs. Hammond arrived home, Betty dropped her work and went to meet her.

"We had a caller," she said. "Miss Ivy Dorset. I was rude. In fact, I was insolent."

"Ah yes," Mrs. Hammond sighed. "The poisonous Ivy. She has that effect on people. She left a note, by way of Smithers. It's probably about you." She opened the envelope, read the note quickly, and dropped both into a waste basket. "It is."

"Our disagreement seemed to revolve mainly about my refusal to take her little doggie to the bathroom."

"Oh. From her note, I gathered that you were plotting to blow up the house. Well, Ivy presumes too much. I will, of course, let her believe that I have dealt severely with the insurrection, but I do not at all like her habit of making free the households of others. In fact, I do not at all like Ivy, which is an unfortunate thing to have to say about my own prospective daughter-in-law."

Something inside Betty stopped. She knew she had heard aright, but she had to be sure.

"Why, yes," Mrs. Hammond replied to her question. "Ivy and Don have been quietly engaged for several months. They were childhood sweethearts, you see. Then they didn't see each other for years. School, and all that. Finally, about six months ago, they met again — but didn't *you* know that?"

From somewhere out of the depths of herself, Betty dragged up her voice.

"No," she heard it say. "No, I didn't know that."

"Oh," said Mrs. Hammond. Just that one word, like the period at the end of a death sentence. Then, somehow, from far away,

"Betty, you don't look well. Are you all right?"

"I guess … I think … I must have gotten more upset about the dog than I realized."

Mrs. Hammond looked keenly at her.

"Yes, the dog, of course. You'd better go to your room and lie down."

"Thank you. I think I will."

Betty closed the door of her room and sat on the edge of the bed. She sat motionless, stunned. It couldn't be. Not Don. He couldn't have done such a thing to her. He *couldn't* have.

Suddenly hope surged into her. She would call him now, at the lab office. She was sure there was some horrible mistake, which a word from Don could clear up. She'd make a joke of it: "Hear you-all is fixin' to marry up … "

She had to look up the number, because she never called the office. She never bothered him there. There was a delay while the call was held up on the office switchboard. She heard background voices as she waited, heard the operator laughing at something. Then there was a sharp click, and she heard Don's voice.

"Don —" she started to say. Then she realized that he was already talking to someone else, and that she had accidentally been cut in on the wire. And, before the conversation began to make sense, she knew who was on the other end. As though to confirm what she knew, Don spoke the name: "Ivy — "

"But Don," Ivy interrupted, "You've *got* to be free this evening. Tell them their old work can wait — they don't pay you anything there anyway. In fact, if you loved me, I think you'd quit it. How are we going to be married if you're already married to a job?"

"Ivy," Don said, "I've already neglected things more than I should. Three nights this week — "

"Three little nights!" Ivy pouted. "A party where you refused to drink, a play where you refused to laugh, and a private little evening at my place where you refused — "

"Ivy, you don't seem to realize how serious this work is."

"And isn't marriage a serious business? Here I've been away for simply ages, and I find you barricaded up like a monk or something. Are we engaged or aren't we?"

Silence, and then,

"You're right. Marriage is a pretty serious matter. We have a great many things to talk over. Things that have been put off too long already."

"Then I'll see you tonight. The usual place? They make a good old-fashioned."

"All right."

"And in parting, Mr. Hammond — "

There was another sharp click and the line was dead. Dead as the hope that had been in Betty's heart as she dialed the number. Dead as her dreams.

Just before she cradled the phone, Betty heard it cut back to the office noises again. The switchboard girl was still laughing. Laughing as though there was still fun in a world turned to ashes.

CHAPTER NINETEEN

OUTRAGE

NEXT morning Betty told Mrs. Hammond she was leaving. Mrs. Hammond was regretful, but seemed almost to be expecting it.

"I hope you know what you're doing," she said. "Whatever it is that's gone wrong, wouldn't it be wiser to wait a few days? Things might look entirely different soon."

Betty shook her head.

"I'm sorry to leave without notice," she replied. "But my mind is made up. I'll have to leave at once. I'll have my things moved out this afternoon."

She returned to her room and began packing. Soon there was a tap at her door, and Dorothy asked if she might step in.

"Why are you leaving?" she asked.

Betty wondered what there was to tell the girl. What could she tell anyone? That she had fallen victim to one of the oldest games in the book, had made a fool of herself over a man who never had any serious intentions toward her? That she had given her whole being to a man who, if he thought of her at all, was concerned only with getting her out of the way? She had no answer to the girl's question.

"I know why it is," Dorothy said when it was plain that Betty was ignoring the query. "It's about Ivy Dorset and Don. You're in love with him, and you just found out that they're engaged."

"I want you to promise me something, without discussing this any further. I want your word, as my friend, that you will not try to interfere."

"But it's so *wrong*, Betty Ivy's such a — a witch! And she'll chase anything that wears pants! She's not right for Don."

"That's their business. Promise?"

Reluctantly, Dorothy did. Then she asked where Betty planned to go.

"Top secret. And don't try checking on where my things are sent. You'll end up in a storage warehouse."

"You aren't leaving an address? What about mail?"

"I'll phone if I get anxious about it."

"Oh, Betty, I don't want you to go! Why does *everything* have to turn into a mess?"

Impulsively, Betty leaned over and kissed the curly top of the girl's head.

"You're a sweet kitten," she said.

A hotel room was Betty's home for a day or two, and then she moved into an inexpensive rooming house. Once she was settled, she seldom left her room, even for meals. She had no interests, no volition. Nothing seemed worth the effort it took to obtain it. Ambition was dead in her, and she felt overwhelmed by an all-pervading pessimism toward life and the people around her.

She recalled, after several days, that letters relative to her father's affairs might be waiting for her at the Hammond home. And so she telephoned one day and asked to speak with either Mrs. Hammond or her secretary. To her surprise, Dorothy came to the phone.

"I'm the new secretary," Dorothy explained, in a manner which seemed to imply that she was as surprised as anyone else. "I offered to help Mother out for a couple of days, and here I am."

"Good for you," Betty said. "Do you like it?"

"It's more interesting than I expected. And even though Mother doesn't trust me the way she did you, she isn't at all bad to work for. In fact, if she weren't my mother, I'd think she was a swell boss. Maybe even some kind of a genius."

"You'll find that she gets smarter as you get older. That's one of the remarkable characteristics of parents."

She inquired about letters and learned that there were a handful.

"And — Betty, there's something I'd like to talk over with you," Dorothy said, dropping her voice. "I can't discuss it on the phone, and I'd rather we didn't talk here. Can I meet you some place?"

Betty didn't want to talk to anyone, really. But there was a tone of real urgency in the girl's voice. And, after going out of her way to win the girl's friendship, it would have been a shabby thing to turn her away now. With some reluctance she named a tea-room where they could meet.

CHAPTER TWENTY

DRESS AND UNDRESS

BETTY took her letters from Dorothy, glanced through them, and put them away as the waitress came to take their order. "Well, Dot, what's the big news?" she asked.

Dorothy waited until the waitress was out of earshot.

"I've so many things I want to say that I don't know where to begin. I'll start with this: Don must have tried to call you after you left. That same night, that is. Either that or Mother called him and in while they were talking. He was excited—I could tell by the way the phone was squawking. It takes a lot to get Don excited. He was shouting, 'Why didn't someone tell me Ivy had been there?', and Mother told him that if he was enough of a damn fool to mishandle his affairs so badly he deserved whatever he got. Then she noticed me and waited politely for me to get out of the room, just as though I were still a kid. So I had to show that *I* knew something about what was going on too, and I said, 'When he hires the detectives to look for her, have him tell them not to bother with the truckers. Her things are in storage.' That was the end of that round."

A spark of hope stirred in Betty's breast. Was there some explanation which would clear up everything and make the world bright again? Was there something which Don, at this moment, wanted desperately to tell her. And then the spark died, for there was really nothing in what Dorothy had said which could not simply have meant that Don was angry at having been found out in that particular way. Yes, perhaps he had wanted the news to have come to her in another, less brutal way, but it all added up to the same thing. He and Ivy had been engaged. They were still engaged. And there had been time for him to see Ivy almost every night for a week, when he had no time for her.

But Dorothy was going on:

"Then, let's see, it must have been the following Thursday when Don and Ivy were out at the house together. It was at night, and I was sitting out in the garden alone because I felt sort of blue about something. I heard a car drive up, but I didn't pay much attention, and they went into the house. Maybe half an hour later I heard voices coming my way, and then I recognized them. I was sitting in a shadow by the hedge, and I didn't want to have to explain what I was mooning about, so I just stayed there and hoped they'd pass on by. But they stopped near me, and they were half-quarreling. I couldn't hear what Don said, but every once in a while Ivy would get excited and raise her voice. She said something about you and Don having been in some town up state when he was supposed to be alone on his vacation, and she called you a few names which I won't repeat, but the mildest one was 'tramp'. Don rumbled something, and she said, 'That's what *you* think. Well, perhaps I'll prove it to you one of these days!' Then there was some more name-calling, and they started away, and all I heard her say after that was, 'Why don't you ask Bobby Morgan?'"

"Dorothy," Betty said in a voice that was tired, "let's just drop the subject for now. I know you are trying to help me, but the best thing you can do is forget the entire thing. Besides, I have a feeling that there's something else on your mind. You haven't told me anything yet which couldn't have been said on the phone."

Dorothy's face grew cautious, and she studied Betty over her teacup. Then, like a gambler who decides to stake everything, she said:

"Betty, I'm in trouble. Bad trouble."

"Oliver Marks?"

Dorothy shook her head. "Only indirectly. Not the way you're thinking. That wouldn't be trouble. At least, not compared to this. The only reason I've come to you about it is because you know Bobby Morgan. Maybe you can talk to him or — or something. It's about him. I was a fool, Betty. An awful fool. I still can't believe — "

"You can bawl yourself out later," Betty said. "Start at the beginning."

"I've known Bobby Morgan for almost a year, now. That is, I always knew him slightly, but it was about a year ago that I started running around to parties and things where he turned up. That was with an entirely different bunch of people from the ones Oliver knows. An older crowd. And faster. A lot faster. I was about the youngest one of the lot, and I felt pretty sophisticated to be moving with them. It flattered the pants off me — and I guess you can take that literally if you want to."

She looked doubtfully at Betty, said, "Bum joke," and continued with her story.

"Oliver didn't like those people, but that didn't bother me too much. I liked him better than anyone I knew, but I was still playing the field. And it seemed to me that the people around Bobby were — oh, like big league players next to a bunch of sandlot kids.

"Somehow I managed to stay out of any real trouble for a long time. And I think I ought to say right here that I never really liked Bobby. He just happened to be around where the fun was going on. Then things began to get serious between Oliver and me. I mean really serious. We — but that isn't part of the story. Anyway, I kept going out with this other crowd whenever I felt like it. Oliver objected, but I told him that he wasn't going to run my life. There were enough people trying to run it already.

"Early this summer things really began to sizzle. Something had happened which made Oliver think that I shouldn't be seeing anyone but him. I didn't see it that way, and every time he said something about the other bunch I'd break my next date with him and go off with them instead. And then Bobby started to chase me."

She began breaking off bits of bread crumb and rolling them into pellets. Betty poured more tea for both of them.

"I don't mean," said Dorothy, "that he called me up at home or anything like that. But at parties he'd try to get me off alone. If we went someplace in a car, he'd try to arrange for me to sit next to him. You know what I mean. I knew what he wanted, and I knew that I didn't want that — not with him. But if there was a crowd

"Well, I couldn't. On one of the first nights warm enough so that along I felt that I could handle things.

we could swim, a few of us ended up at Bobby's cabin on Hell's Drop. That is, he calls it a cabin, but it's more of a ranch house. I suppose you know the place — on that point with the cliff falling off to the sea on one side and a path winding down to the beach and the dock on the other."

Betty had never seen the place, but she did not say so.

"I knew only a couple of the people in the party," Dorothy said, "and I should have left when they did — when things began to get rough. You see, one of the fellows had a can of ether on him, and they started passing it around and — were you ever on an ether jag?"

"No. I missed that."

"Well, don't bother to try it. I can't describe it. It's sort of a dream world. Everything changes. I wasn't going to touch the stuff, but when another girl refused it and started to make a fuss somebody said, 'Don't bother with that square. Pass it on to Dotty — she's hep.' And I had to go ahead and pretend that I was an old hand at that sort of thing, just to be smart. Next thing I knew, everything in the world was wonderfully funny, and I was ready for anything, almost. When somebody suggested a dip, I was ready for that. And when Bobby said that he didn't have any suits in the place, but that it was dark enough to go in without any, I thought that was all right too. Actually, there was a full moon, but everybody went down to the beach, except those who were already too knocked out to move. And then we took our clothes off and went in.

"Even though everybody was pretty high, most of them seemed a little embarrassed and stayed near the water at first. Some of the women, though, hardly got wet. They just paraded back and forth, trying to get people to look at them. One girl, who had been the loudest in backing the suggestion in the first place, changed her mind when she got to the beach, and refused to undress. A bunch of men and women alike chased her around until they caught her, and then they stripped her and threw her in the water. I laughed as much as the rest. Everything was still getting funnier and funnier.

"Then somebody discovered that Bobby was taking pictures. He's sort of an amateur photographer, even though most of the things he takes are just cruel little snapshots of people in situations where they look awkward or ugly. He was using that infrared film, the kind which is sensitive to coated flash bulbs that don't give any light that you can see, and it was a long time before he was discovered. When they found out what ht was doing, it all was a great joke, but they started after him to get the film, and Bobby ran up to the house and that sort of broke up the swimming party.

"Things begin to get hazy there. I just can't remember everything. I seemed to get lost in ether fumes, and then I felt terribly sick and someone was helping me into another room. I started toward a couch, and then I was in darkness, falling and falling and falling, spinning and never stopping. When I woke up it was daylight. I was on the couch, and my clothes were on the floor on the other side of the room. I felt awful.

"I dressed and went into a bathroom and bathed my face with cold water until I felt a little better. I was sick physically, and I was sick with myself. The place was a mess. There were people passed out or sleeping all over the house, and in all conditions of dress and undress. There was even a naked woman snoring away in the bathtub where someone had tried to bring her around with a shower and given it up. I tiptoed over people and went out to my car. I was shaking like a leaf, and I could hardly get the key into the ignition. Driving away, I almost ran over a man who came staggering out of the woods where he had evidently slept all night."

Betty saw that she was expected to make some comment.

"Quite an experience," she said. "I should think that would have finished you with that bunch."

"You'd think so. But it didn't. Oh, I kept away from them for a while. I didn't think I could ever face any of those people again. But when I ran into any of them they acted just as they always had. somebody was complaining that he had lost his wristwatch in the In fact, the only reference to that night I ever heard was when water. So, gradually, I started going around with them sometimes, and nothing like that ever happened again.

"But Bobby began to bother me more after that. He wanted me to go out alone with him, and I wouldn't do it. And he began making remarks that I didn't understand. He'd say things like, 'After all, in view of what happened after our swimming party...', and then leave me hanging, wondering what he was talking about. Then, one night at a party he took me aside and showed me a picture taken at the beach. I was in it — stark naked, with my arms draped over the shoulder of a man I don't even remember."

The girl closed her eyes and shook her head in a gesture that told, more than words could have, how much the memory cost her.

"I was scared. Panicky. You can imagine how I felt. I hadn't mentioned the party to Oliver, of course, and if he saw something like that — I asked Bobby to give me the picture, and, surprisingly enough, he burned it in an ashtray. He became very sweet and understanding and said he'd give me all the pictures I was in, and the negatives too. I was so bowled over that I told him how things were between Oliver and me, that we were going to be married and all, and he patted my wrist and said he understood and not to worry about a thing. We made a date to meet at a bar next day, when he would give me the rest of the pictures.

"When I kept the date I found him looking very grave, and he made a big production over getting a booth where we couldn't be overheard. He acted so funny that I was sure something had gone wrong. I couldn't wait to get my hands on the prints. There weren't any negatives — he said that he had burned them. And then he said, in a very odd way, '*Those* aren't the ones you have to worry about.'"

Reaching into her handbag, Dorothy handed an envelope to Betty.

"Before I go any further, you might as well look at these. Yes," she insisted as Betty raised her brows, "you might as well. I daresay you aren't the only person who's seen them. And I'm sure Bobby didn't destroy those negatives."

Betty thumbed through the half dozen prints. As Dorothy had pointed out, Bobby Morgan's photography was not pretty. The delicate features of the girl across the table had been transformed into something almost bestially lewd. Intoxicated as she had been, her face was slack, distorted, and shockingly brutalized. Dorothy, watching Betty, clenched her small fists and said,

"Go ahead, say it. Tell me what you see. I've heard the word before."

"I see a very foolish girl," Betty said. Thinking of her own experience with the man, she added, "I'm not condoning what you've done. But you're not the first foolish girl to get into a scrape. Surely something can be done about it. If you think Bobby still has the negatives, the best thing you can do is go to Oliver and tell him the whole story. That may seem difficult, but it's the only thing, under the circumstances. Together, you and he should be able to plan how to handle Bobby Morgan. And don't worry about Oliver not believing it was exactly as you've explained it to me. If he loves you, he will. And if necessary I can tell him a thing or two about Bobby Morgan myself."

"You don't know Oliver very well," Dorothy said. "Why should he believe me now, when I've been deceiving him all along? Besides, that's not the worst of it. God, if it only were!"

With fingers that trembled she lighted a cigarette and inhaled deeply, so that when she spoke little clouds of smoke bubbled out with her words.

"When Bobby said, 'Those aren't the ones you have to worry about,' I knew something really dreadful was going to happen. He acted surprised when I asked what he meant. He said he was talking about the pictures that had been taken in the room I woke up in. *Pictures somebody else had taken!*

"I told him I didn't know anything about any other pictures — that I didn't remember a thing after I got into the room. He hemmed and hawed and acted evasive and pretended not to believe me. *He* hadn't known about it at the time, he said, or he wouldn't have allowed it, but from what he had heard, I had thought it was a big joke at the time. Then he showed me — these."

A second envelope was passed across the table. One glance brought the blood tingling to Betty's face. She riffled through a few of them and, skipping the rest, returned them to the envelope. She had heard of such pictures — of such things — but it was almost impossible to believe that Dorothy…

"Bobby claimed that someone he barely knew had taken the pictures and had sent them to him. He said it was an out-and-out blackmail set up. The fellow was supposed to be some college student who was hard up for money to pay gambling debts, and he wanted Bobby to get in touch with me and tell me the pictures were for sale. He was sure Bobby would do it because the pictures were taken at his place, so he'd be involved too. I asked who it was, and he said he couldn't tell me the name — for my own protection! Because if it all wasn't handled very carefully the fellow would see to it that prints were sent to Oliver — and Oliver's mother.

"I was frantic. I started to cry, and Bobby played a sympathy gag and said he thought he might be able to fix it up without paying blackmail. Or, if he couldn't do that, he'd pay the fellow off himself, because all I have is an allowance, and I could never get hold of the kind of money that was involved. Then he wanted me to go to his apartment in Manhattan and talk it all over.

"I'm no genius, but I began to catch on. There was no other fellow. Those pictures came from Bobby himself, and he was using them to get me to sleep with him. I accused him of it, and he denied it, of course, but he did say that sleeping with him couldn't be such a high price to pay after — after *that*.

"And Betty, the worst of it is, I don't know! I can't remember a thing after I passed out. I can't believe that I ever did such a thing. I don't remember those three men or — anything. But that's the room, and there's no doubt about it being me, and — oh God, Betty, I don't know what I'm going to do! This has been going on for weeks, now, and Bobby is getting nastier and more insistent all the time. He tells me that this 'other person' won't wait forever, and he finally came out and put it on a blunt, business basis. One night at Hell's Drop in exchange for the pictures. In other words, I'm to become a whore if I want to keep any part of my happiness with Oliver. And I love Oliver, truly, so much, so much … And we have such a lovely life planned, and I know that all I want in the world is Oliver! Betty, if you have any influence with Bobby, if there's anything you can do, help me, help me! Call me anything you like, despise me, but please, if there's any way you can, help me now!"

Dorothy's voice was rising, and one or two people glanced in their direction. Betty, seeing that the girl's nerves were on the verge of snapping, signaled for the check.

"Let's go for a ride," she said. "Somewhere out in the country."

Betty handled the wheel of the little Jaguar while Dorothy, huddled in the seat beside her, closed her eyes and let the tears run down her cheeks to be washed away by the wind. They drove for several miles in silence, and then Betty pulled up under a line of huge maples which stretched their leafy branches over the narrow, little-traveled road.

"Betty," Dorothy pleaded after several more silent minutes, "say something. Anything. Anything is better than this silence between us."

"I don't know what to say," Betty slowly declared, "The beach pictures were one thing. But this other ... "

"I know. Do you think I don't feel the same way about it? It's monstrous. Horrible. I suppose I should be glad that I can't remember. I don't even recognize the men. And I don't know what to do!"

"Bobby Morgan seems to have the solution," Betty suggested, watching Dorothy from the corner of her eye.

"I won't do it!" the girl almost screamed. "I love Oliver, and I won't go to bad with Bobby, no matter what! He'll go through with his threat, I know he will — and that will be the end of it. And me. Do you think I could live after that, after the disgrace to my family, after the news columns start hinting about it? If I lose Oliver, I don't want to live. I know that sounds corny, but the other night I took a razor blade and — it wouldn't be hard. Not as hard as living like this."

A flash of gold and black swooped down and settled on the hood of the car, its beads of eyes watchful as the head flicked from side to side.

"Betty, didn't you ever in your life make a mistake about something — someone?"

"Yes." Betty's eyes followed the bird as it darted off into the free sky. "Yes, I have made bad mistakes. But that doesn't mean that I know how to help you."

Dorothy's despair was like a tangible physical force about them. She did not look like a girl now. She looked like a little old woman who has been beaten down by a lifetime of forces too great to be fought.

"Then there's only one thing left to try," Dorothy said. "Don. I don't know how I'll do it, but I'll have to tell Don."

"Don't do that," Betty said quickly.

"What else is there to do now? He'll know about it eventually — good God, he'll be involved in the mess when it comes out. And maybe, just maybe, he might know what to do."

Betty's mind was back in a small office in the Deep Sea Club. The flash of a shot, a face splitting like a melon under Don's murderous fists ...

Murderous. Don's temper, once out of hand, was such that he could come dangerously close to killing, even though he had never seen the men before. If it were a Bobby Morgan, someone whom he actively despised, against whom he bore an old grudge — and if Dorothy were involved ... The story Dorothy had to tell was so sickeningly sordid that it could not do otherwise than move any man to rage. When that man was Don, the only result could be —

"Murder," she said aloud.

"What?" Dorothy asked.

"Dorothy, you mustn't tell Don."

"Musn't I? Then what must I do? You can't help me. No one else can help me. No, if it's to be anyone, it will have to be Don."

"Maybe I can do something. I can try anyway. But I haven't seen Bobby Morgan lately, and I'm afraid I don't have his phone numbers."

Eagerly, Dorothy gave her half a dozen numbers representing Bobby's residences and clubs.

"And those photographs," Betty said as she capped her pen. "It isn't wise for you to keep them. Better let me have them."

They were handed over.

"And now," Betty said, "let's dry our tears and get back to town."

Dorothy tried to smile.

"You really think everything will be all right, somehow?"

"Yes," Betty said as she slid the car into gear. "Everything will be all right. Somehow."

CHAPTER TWENTY-ONE

FECUND MYSTERY

THE phone was silent for a moment after Betty identified herself. Then Bobby's laugh, a little incredulous, came surging over the wire.

"Betty Brooks! This *is* a surprise! Just finished your dip, I suppose?"

"I'd like to talk to you," Betty said, trying to keep her dislike of the man out of her voice. "It's rather important."

"And I should like to talk to you, also," Bobby agreed. "It was very naughty of you to leave my party like that."

"This is about another matter. Something which I think you can clear up very easily."

"Oh?" Bobby sounded more wary.

"When can we discuss it? It's something which can't be handled over the phone."

"I'm sure it can't — if you say not. Still, I feel that I would like to have some idea what it's about."

"It's about a friend of mine. Dorothy Hammond. She's in a bit of trouble, and she told me that you had — had offered to help her. I though we might get together and see if we couldn't expedite matters somewhat."

There was a lengthy pause, and then Bobby said, "Yes, Dotty told me something about some difficulty. I didn't know you two were quite so friendly."

"Then we can do something about this?"

"Why don't we meet somewhere tonight?" Bobby evaded. "I'm not doing anything important. Say, an hour from now?"

"Where?"

"Do you know a bar called The Little Red Rooster?"

"No, but I'll find it. In an hour."

"Wear your best smile," said Bobby as he rang off.

Prompt to the minute, Betty walked into the place an hour later, to find Bobby already lounging at the bar. He summoned a waiter at once, and they were led into the dining room and to a half-hidden, dimly lighted booth in one corner. Bobby was drinking scotch on the rocks; Betty went along with the scotch, but ordered it with soda — plenty of soda.

"I had almost forgotten what a lovely creature you really are," Bobby said. "When you came to mind, I just couldn't believe what my memory told me about you."

Betty said something lightly deprecatory and polite. Had she been told, after that night on Bobby's yacht, that another night would find her seated alone in a bar with him, to all appearances quite friendly as they drank together, it would have seemed incredible. Yet here she was, swallowing her pride and trying to be normally pleasant as Bobby glibly offered his exaggerated compliments and smiled at her in a way which attempted to imitate friendliness.

She had to, she told herself. There was too much at stake for her to allow her true feelings to be seen. Dorothy, in her foolishness, had unwittingly contrived a situation of tremendously explosive possibilities. Mishandled, it could, at the very least, lead to a disgraceful public scandal involving the entire Hammond family. And at worse — at worst, it could lead to Don's standing trial for Bobby's murder. For in Betty's mind there was no doubt that Don was quite capable of killing the man who had destroyed his sister.

She remembered a night when she and Don had been sitting at a campfire and the conversation had touched briefly on Don's search for Dorothy on Bobby's yacht.

"It's that damn temper of mine," he had said. "I shouldn't have brought Dot's name into it at all, with half a dozen people listening. But I looked at that fatuous grin of his, and I couldn't help myself. I told him that if he didn't leave her alone, I'd kill him."

"Very foolish," Betty had replied.

"I know it. The trouble is that, given the right conditions, I might very well do it."

At the time, Betty had passed this off as a meaningless exaggeration. Now, though, since she had seen him lose his temper, she didn't doubt it for an instant. And so she managed to smile as Bobby, with bits of small talk and gossip, tried to live up to his reputation of being utterly fascinating to women.

But why, after what had passed between Donald and herself, should she be doing this? It was an embarrassing — a humiliating position in which to place herself. For friendship with Dorothy? Well, she had grown to like the girl tremendously. Remembering her past, the years after her father's death, she knew all too well what a sympathetic older friend could have meant sometimes — had there been one. Dorothy's whole happiness hinged on the outcome of this matter — and it was not too much to assume that her life might also, for in her present state her threats to take her own life might not be passed over lightly.

The real reason, though, and well she knew it, was that she still loved Don. Yes, in spite of the very wrong thing he had done her, in spite of the pain which she was sure would never die, she loved him. She had given herself, all, in faith that she would always love him. She would not even try to kill that love, not ever. Don had not been quite all that she thought. But he was still Don, and for that she would always be his. And Don must not be allowed to destroy himself in a moment of blind rage. Dorothy was too hysterical to see that. So panicky that she could not reason, Dorothy was capable of touching off the spark which could result only in tragedy.

Bobby was saying something about a recent hill-climbing race in which he had won second place with a 1914 Stutz Bearcat from his collection of antique cars. He interrupted himself to order another round of drinks, and then Betty broke in.

"Can we get down to the real reason I'm here?" she asked. "I'd like to get it over with."

"But of course." Bobby spread his hands in a gesture to indicate his complete openness. "I've simply been waiting for you to bring it up."

"Very well. When I say that Dorothy has told me about her trouble, we both know what I mean. To make it short, I know about the pictures, and I'm here to see what can be done about them."

"I see." Bobby rolled the ice in his glass. "Then, if she has told you the whole story, you must realize that it's a very delicate situation. I'm afraid Dorothy's — er, pursuit of happiness went a bit out of bounds. Not that I object to anyone else's idea of fun, you understand. But to allow herself to be photographed like that — very indiscreet, to say the least. I didn't know about it myself, or I would, of course, have put a stop to it. As it is, Dorothy has placed both herself and me in a rather bad spot. The fellow who has the pictures is getting nasty, and I'm afraid he means business. He's calling me every day, now. Personally, you realize, my position isn't too bad. I can't really be accountable for the misbehavior of my guests. And another little flare-up in the papers wouldn't be a novelty to me. The fellow knows that, so he's trying to use me as a go-between while he bleeds Dorothy."

Betty looked him squarely in the eye, and he stared back. A few accomplished liars are able to do that.

"And for the return of the pictures this — person — wants how much?"

"Twenty-five thousand dollars. Considering the family he's dealing with, I think he's being very easy on the girl."

It was so neatly clever, Betty thought. Of course Bobby was no blackmailer — not for money. Why should he be, when he had more than he knew how to spend? And the sum was so ridiculously small in comparison with his millions that, had anyone dared to accuse him, the accusation would have been laughed away as obvious nonsense. At the same time, twenty-five thousand dollars was an impossible sum for Dorothy. For all their wealth, the Hammonds had not raised their children to be wastrels. Dorothy was allowed an amount adequate to allow her to dress well and to travel in the circle of her kind. It was doubtful that she could lay her hands on more than a thousand dollars in actual cash. The alternative was simple — to sell herself to Bobby in the guise of being grateful to him for paying off the blackmailer himself. To Bobby this whole thing was only an elaborate game played for his own amusement, with Dorothy as the prize. At least, such was the case if Dorothy was right in believing that Bobby himself was engineering the entire scheme — and Betty herself felt that he was.

She decided to bluff.

"Suppose the money is produced right now — how soon can the arrangements be made? Can I get the pictures tonight?"

Bobby blinked, and Betty knew that the possibility of Dorothy somehow getting the money was something he had neither considered nor desired.

"I wouldn't go so far as to say that," he cautiously evaded. "As I told you, the whole thing is very delicate. These things take time."

"I thought you said this person was in a hurry. Phoning you every day. Yet now that you hear that his demands can be met, he suddenly isn't in a hurry at all Why? What are you trying to hide?"

"But my dear Betty, *I* have nothing to hide," Bobby protested.

"Then prove it. If things are as you say, you should be anxious to get this over with as quickly as possible. Tonight."

Bobby frowned. "It isn't so easy as you might believe. I *could* try to get in touch with this fellow, I suppose. He gave me a number to call ... "

"Then call it. Tell him Dorothy has agreed to his terms — but only if the exchange can be made tonight. If he tries to hold out for more, she'll go to the police."

"Dorothy won't go to the police," Bobby said meaningfully. "But I'll see what I can do."

He walked out toward the bar where the phone booths were, pausing on the way to reorder from the waiter.

While she was waiting, Betty's mind busily raced over the possibilities. Her bluff seemed to be working. If Bobby himself had the pictures, the last thing in the world which he wanted was to have someone actually pay him money for them. That would have made the game just a bit too dangerous. If she could just make her bluff stick, he would probably make some last-minute pretense of paying the black-mailer himself, and be glad to be rid of the whole thing. On the other hand, if there actually was someone else, and she could meet that person, she had a good chance of getting her hands on the negatives before it was discovered that she could not pay. She knew that Bobby was lying, at least in part, but he had managed to confuse things in such a way that she was not sure how much might be the truth after all. The important thing was to gain possession of the film, and to do that she'd just have to keep one step ahead of Bobby, pretending to be a little bit suspicious — but not too suspicious of everything.

Bobby came back, giving the appearance of a man preoccupied.

"What luck?" Betty asked.

"I found him. And made an appointment for tonight."

"Where? At what time?"

"My cabin at Hell's Drop. I don't know exactly when. Within the next couple of hours. We're to drive out and wait for him."

"That doesn't sound promising at all. Why should he want to go all the way out there when he could have met us in this place, or one like it?"

"*I* don't pretend to read minds. We are dealing with a blackmailer, remember. He probably has perfectly good reasons."

"I don't like it."

"No more do I. Please bear in mind that *you* came to *me* with this problem. I can't say that I particularly care for any part of it. And I'd like to add that I think Dorothy was very unwise to complicate matters by bringing another person into the *dramatis per-*

"She's much too upset to handle it herself," Betty said quickly. *sonae.*"

"Don't you think that, since we're both involved in this, I ought to know something about how you two became such good friends?"

"I've been working as her mother's secretary. Since we were living under the same roof and were thrown together a lot — well, we just grew to know each other rather intimately."

"You can't wonder that I'm surprised. After the wet blanket you threw on my yachting party, acting Ike a school-marm as you did, to find you so intimate with a girl who — but need I go further?"

The insolent coolness with which he indicated that he saw no fault in his own conduct brought a sharp answer to the tip of Betty's tongue, but without waiting for a reply Bobby glanced at his watch, tossed off hit drink, and said,

"I suppose we ought to be leaving."

"I — I suppose so."

When she stood up, Betty found that her knees were trembling. She didn't want to go to Bobby's cabin. She didn't want to be anywhere near him, and she was frightened. But she had to go through with it now. Had to, for Dorothy and for Don, even though neither of them could ever know all of the truth...

Then, just as they were leaving, Chance stepped in to further twist the tangled skein from which the pattern of Betty's life was being knit. A car drew up to the curb and parked. Instantly, Betty recognized Don's convertible. Then, as Bobby led her toward his own car, Don and Ivy came down the street.

Betty's heart turned over. With all of herself she longed to rush up to him, to touch his hand, even to throw herself wildly into his arms and claim him for her own. But that was insane, not at all the sort of thing civilized people did. And she knew that she could not trust herself to greet him, to nod and speak to him quietly, while that other woman clung possessively to his elbow.

Chattering nonsense, she directed Bobby's attention to a window display of lamps, watching the other couple from the corner of her eye. Ivy was speaking forcefully to Don, and they seemed about to pass without looking up. Then Don's glance wandered, and Betty quickly averted her face. Feeling his eyes upon her, hearing the rhythm of his stride break, she clutched Bobby's arm with a show of gaiety and hurried by. Bobby never even noticed the couple, though they all but brushed his shoulder. A corner was turned, and the moment was passed.

That bar, then, must be "the usual place", Betty realized as she dropped into the deep, leopard-covered seat of Bobby's car. By chance she had been led to the very spot where Don's meetings with Ivy had taken place — perhaps they had even occupied the same table! And now she could know that tonight, while she tried to unravel Dorothy's affairs without involving Don, he was with Ivy, probably relieved that she had failed to recognize him and embarrass him before his fiancee. It was all so idiotic that she laughed aloud.

"You seem to be in a sudden good mood," Bobby observed as he kicked the engine into roaring life.

"Who wouldn't be? Everything is wonderful. Just wonderful. And crazy. I feel like *Alice in Wonderland*. No, *Through the Looking Glass*. Everything is turned inside out."

As Bobby's flashy car passed the bar, she saw Don and Ivy again. Ivy, at the door of the place, had turned impatiently. Don, his face a blank mask, was watching them drive by, and he did not move as Ivy came up to him. Looking in the rear-view mirror, Betty saw him standing there, staring, until another car blocked her view.

Something that was half a sob, half a giggle, escaped her lips. Now that Don had seen her with Bobby, his own conscience was probably greatly eased. He could tell himself that all she had wanted him to believe about herself was a vast, contrived lie, that she had really been, all the time, just another of Bobby Morgan's chippies, and that he was lucky to be free of her.

"What's going on with you?" Bobby asked as he stopped for a traffic light. "You're certainly not having hysterics, but I can't decide whether you're laughing or crying. Is something wrong?"

Betty dabbed at the corners of her eyes and shook her head.

"I was just thinking of something terribly funny. One of those private jokes. No, nothing's wrong. Everything is just as perfectly right as it could possibly be. Let's have some music. How do you turn on the radio in this maze of gadgets?"

Bobby pointed out the proper controls and then added, "There's a bottle of good Irish whiskey in the glove compartment."

Irish whiskey."

"That's fine," Betty said. "Just what I need. A bottle of good

She tuned the radio and pressed the button to open the glove compartment.

"None for me," Bobby said as she offered the bottle. "Not just yet."

The bottle tilted.

"Sure?" Betty wiped her lips.

"When we're out of town. Don't hold back on my account. I'm glad to see you let down your hair and act a little more human for a change."

"I'm going to be a lot more human," Betty said, "from now on."

The bottle tilted once more before the compartment latch snapped.

Bobby slowed for the curve as they turned onto a dirt road, then rolled to a quiet stop.

"Why are we stopping here?" Betty asked. "We have an appointment to keep."

"Time for me to have a drink too. You can't handle *all* of that bottle."

"Oh. Here."

"You first."

Betty had lost track of the number of times she had taken the bottle from its resting place. It was a very friendly bottle, she thought. It couldn't help her forget the picture of Ivy and Don coming arm in arm down the street, but it made the idea more bearable. It helped to detach her from things, so that she could stand aside and look at them from another angle. It seemed to give her a better perspective. About everything.

What was the difference, for instance, between a Bobby Morgan and a Donald Hammond? Neither of them could really help being what he was. Bobby was out for what he could get, and so, it appeared, was Don. But Donald pretended that he was something else. Don was very much shocked by the way Bobby Morgan acted, when all the time, all the time ...

"Hey," said Bobby, "how about me?"

"Sorry." Betty handed over the bottle. If only the radio would stop playing those damn, saccharin love songs! They were so terribly stupid and childish — and somehow they hurt, especially the older ones.

"Have you really changed?" Bobby was asking, "or is it just that we're getting to know each other better?"

He was glancing down at her knee. Betty saw, in the dim light of the dash panel, that her skirt had become disarranged and pulled rather high on her silk-clad thigh. She started to tug it down, but it didn't seem to matter as much as it should have. She was after those negatives, she reminded herself. It wouldn't hurt to pretend to flirt with Bobby, lead him on, while she kept a clear head, a clear head ...

"I think I'm beginning to know myself better," she replied. "I seem to know a lot of things I didn't know before."

Bobby's arm went across the back of the seat as he stretched. Then his fingers dropped lightly to her shoulder. They rested there motionless, only to begin a restless, spidery movement after a moment. He touched her neck, the back of her ear, her cheek ...

"Shouldn't we be going on?" Betty asked uneasily.

"Plenty of time," Bobby assured her. "My place isn't far from here. And don't you think that, since we've decided to be friends, we ought to kiss and make up?"

"I'm sure we could do without such formalities," Betty nervously laughed.

Instead of replying, Bobby drew her toward himself, turning her resisting head to bring her face to his. Then his lips were on hers, moist and eager, and pressing hard. Betty writhed in his embrace, trying to struggle free. In the next instant, though, her will to resist was strangely weakened.

For, what did it really matter? A kiss, an unwelcome caress to be briefly endured so that she might easier accomplish what she had set out to do, that was all it was. And for whose sake was she placing such a premium on her kisses? Don? How highly he valued them was quite plainly evident. Right now, for all she knew, he might be kissing Ivy. Like this. And — like this.

Her mood changed like a scattering breeze, and she pulled away.

"Well!" Bobby said. "That's what I call real southern hospitality. Let's try some more of that."

This time Betty brushed aside his hand and pulled down her skirt with definite finality.

"Let's keep that appointment," she said.

Reluctance was on Bobby's face as he put the car in gear, but he did not object. She was quite able, Betty now felt, to keep the situation in control. It was quite easy to handle Bobby Morgan, if only one pretended to play along with his game.

CHAPTER TWENTY-TWO
PAYMENT ON DELIVERY

S OME part of Betty's earlier sense of misgiving returned as she and Bobby left his car and approached the dark, brooding structure which he referred to as his "cabin". After what had happened to her on the yacht, it was a foolhardy risk she was taking. For here they were truly alone. There were no servants, of course, and she assumed that the nearest neighbors must be miles away. It was no easy thing for her to step into a pitch-black and strange room with him, but she made herself do it as though it were the most natural thing in the world. A snap of a switch flooded the place with light, driving away some of her apprehension, and she found that the cabin was just what one might have expected of Bobby Morgan. It was a place for people to pretend that they were roughing it, apparently decorated by a designer whose effete notions of rusticity had been developed in Hollywood via a careful study of the pages of the magazines *Flair* and *Esquire.* From the artificially-aged beams which supported nothing, to the wood-pegged, but expensively-upholstered chairs, the whole was an elaborate fake, a somewhat labored imitation of something more robust. Betty could almost imagine the decorator pasting false hair on his chest before he set to work.

Bobby took her things and began bustling about. As always with him, the first consideration was to look to the liquor supply, and glasses and ice were soon tinkling on the huge slab of

J.T. PRITCHARD

red-wood which was a coffee table. He shivered as he handled a chilled soda bottle, and rubbed his hands briskly.

"Brrr! The nights get cold early here. I think we could use a bit of a fire to take off the chill. No use turning on the central heating."

The over-sized fireplace worked, at least, and soon a dancing blaze was spreading its warmth throughout the place. Bobby toyed with a radio disguised in a pine cabinet of Revolutionary vintage, and settled himself on the couch beside Betty, casually flicking ashes onto the largest Navajo rug Betty had ever seen. She looked at her watch and said,

"When do you think we can expect your — friend?"

"You know as much as I do. Let's not make ourselves nervous worrying about it. There are many more enjoyable ways of spend-the evening. I can think of several right now."

"I didn't expect this affair to be a pleasure excursion, exactly. It's a serious matter. To Dorothy it's damned serious."

"Of course. But I'm sure everything will turn out all right."

He refilled Betty's glass, which she had already emptied without realizing it. Then, moving closer, he slid his arm around her waist.

"You mustn't let other people's troubles bother you so much. You have your own life to live. You're young, beautiful — you ought to be enjoying the things life has to offer you. Things could be very different for you, Betty, if you'd only let yourself go."

My own life to live, Betty was thinking. A whole lifetime to live — without Don. While Ivy, who took her pleasure where she found it, whose way of life was that of Bobby's crowd, blithely added Don to the collection of things she wanted — and took as her right.

"For instance," Bobby went on, "you could have had a wonderful week on that cruise, if only you hadn't been so foolish. Life is short, Betty,and we have to grab at whatever fun is offered. And it wouldn't hurt you a bit to have friends like the people you were meeting. Some of them might turn out to be very useful someday."

"I — I suppose you're right," she said. "But do we have to talk about me?"

"I can't think of anything I'd rather talk about. But if you say no talk — no talk."

He put down his drink and inched himself closer. His breath fell hotly against her neck as he bent to kiss her partly bare shoulder, and at the same time his hand dropped to her knee, disturbing her skirt. Betty jerked her leg away, starting so violently that her own drink splashed over her stockings and the hem of her dress.

"Sorry," Bobby said, whipping out a handkerchief and dabbing at the spreading wet patches. "I didn't expect you to be so skittish."

"Ugh!" Betty said, standing and shaking at her skirt. "I can't stand wet stockings."

"Then take them off, by all means. They'll dry quickly by the fire."

"I'm afraid I'll have to. They're soaked. Is there a bedroom I can use?"

"Little Miss Modesty! No need for that, you know."

"If you don't mind, I'd rather — "

"I'm busy elsewhere," Bobby sighed, and he turned his back.

Betty hesitated, then settled back on the couch and turned back her dress. With her fine, long legs thrust out before her, she quickly unhooked her garters and stripped off the offending stockings. She had them in her hand and was slipping back into her shoes when she happened to glance in the direction of Bobby's gaze. He was looking at a window which was so located that it offered a perfect mirror. Their eyes met, and he grinned triumphantly. Blood rushed to Betty's cheeks, and she bit her lip to hold back an angry protest. Then Bobby took the stockings and hung them by the fireplace.

"Rather early to expect Old Kris Kringle," he observed. "But you never can tell."

He came back to the couch and sat down again, this time sitting sideways, so that he and Betty faced each other.

"I believe I was about to kiss you again," he declared.

Betty's objection was cut off by the smothering wrench of his mouth on hers. She resisted, but only briefly. For what, she wondered, did it really matter now? Whether she allowed or refused Bobby's kisses was of not the slightest importance to anyone. If kissing Bobby was part of the game, she would kiss him. She would get a bit tight, too, if she felt like it. Maybe she already was, just a little. The thing was, in this world you were supposed to get what you went after, and the way to get what she wanted from Bobby Morgan was — like this.

She felt the warm touch of his hands. Let it be that way, then. So long as she didn't allow him to go too far, that didn't matter either. She lay passive under his caresses, vaguely aware, in some detached way, that her own body was being quickened into a kind of response. And that, she told herself, just went to prove what a farce the whole business of love was. If she could be stirred by a man whom she actually detested, then it was ridiculous to pretend that what had been between Don and her was the precious thing she had believed it.

The room was suddenly warm. She pushed her way to her feet and ran her fingers through her slightly disarranged hair.

The radio gave her an excuse.

"Listen!" she exclaimed. "They're playing some old Goodman arrangements. I haven't heard that for years."

" 'Let's Dance'," Bobby named the title of the tune. "Well, let's."

He swept her into his arms, and they glided smoothly across the room. Bobby danced easily and well. But, like everything else, he made it much more personal than was necessary. The arm which circled her waist held her too tightly. The fingers of their joined hands were interlocked, and their bodies were crushed intimately together. As they danced past a lamp, Bobby paused to snap it out, and a moment later he turned off another, leaving only one dim bulb and the flickering fire to light the long, shadowed room.

More and mere wildly they danced. And now, to Betty, the music appeared to be a part of her. The pulsing beat of her heart sent the blood coursing in hot waves through her body. She could hear it pound in her ears, in almost perfect time to the score. Her body, unconscious of its obedience to Bobby's movements, seemed to act of itself as it carried her lightly to even more intense heights. It was as though she had been caught up in that web of melody and rhythms and must dance on and on and on, madly and ever more madly until something burst to discharge the tension and allow her to fall exhausted.

The fantasy was snapped suddenly as the music came to an end. Feeling much too warm, and somewhat giddy as well, Betty stood swaying slightly as Bobby mopped his brow.

"Phew!" he exclaimed. "Either that arrangement is a lot faster than it was ten years ago, or I'm a lot slower. Another go?"

Betty shook her head and went back to the couch. Now that the music had stopped, her feet seemed less inclined to obey her. The floor appeared to have a tilt which had not been there before.

Bobby was holding another drink for her. She knew she didn't need it, but it looked cool, so she took it. But when Bobby tried to put his arm around her again, she shook it off.

"This isn't what I came for," she said. "Look at the time. I don't see any sign of that person we were supposed to meet."

Bobby took time to select a cigaret from his case, thumb his lighter, and inhale a long drag before he answered.

"Perhaps he isn't coming," he said.

"What do you mean?" Betty sensed that something was going wrong, and her mind struggled to become more alert. "You told me he would be here within two hours!"

"Possibly," Bobby suggested, looking at the glowing end of his cigaret, "possibly he realized that it would be foolish, since he couldn't get what he was after. The objective was twenty-five thousand dollars — and you don't have it."

"He couldn't know — I mean, that's ridiculous!"

"Is it? Very well. Let us count the money to be sure the sum is correct. No use overpaying, you know."

"I — I ..."

"You've been trying to bluff, Betty. But you know, and I know, that Dorothy doesn't have that amount in her own name."

Betty's anger began to well up. Bobby had known all along that she was lying. And he had toyed with her, enjoying this unexpected twist to the vicious game he was playing with Dorothy's life and happiness.

"All right," she flared. "So we both know that I haven't got the money! And we both also know this — that you made no phone call tonight because there is no other person involved, that you, and no one else, have those negatives, and that the whole filthy mess is nothing but a vindictive scheme to force Dorothy to sleep with you!"

"Tut-tut-tut!" Bobby chided. "Such an outburst! I suppose you can prove all this?"

"There's plenty of proof for me! If you haven't got the negatives, how could you promise them to Dorothy in return for going to bed with you? From what I know of you, money may go through your hands like water, but you're not paying off someone else's blackmail out of the kindness of your heart, no matter what that person may have done for you or been to you!"

Bobby smiled to himself.

"If these things were so," he said, " — and mind you, I am not admitting that they are — why should you have to become entangled? you make it sound very simple. Dorothy sleeps with me and gets back her pictures. The pictures in themselves show that she shouldn't have any scruples about a little thing like that. So where is the problem?"

"I'll tell you where the problem is!" Betty almost hissed. "It concerns your own worthless life, so perhaps you'd better listen!

Dorothy isn't the kind of girl those pictures seem to say. I don't know if she was drugged at the time or out of her mind, *but she isn't that sort of a girl!* She won't prostitute herself to you, not even with all the threats you've used to terrify her. But what she will do, if I don't return with those negatives, is tell her brother Donald the whole story. I think you know him well enough to know what that would mean."

"I well remember that he was tactless enough to make a scene and threaten my life not long ago. Are you attempting to use that threat again?"

"No. No, I'm not trying to threaten you. I am simply reminding you that Donald already dislikes you. His temper is such that if Dorothy were to tell him this story — "

Bobby interrupted with a laugh.

"Betty," he said, "your second attempt to bluff is even worse than the first. If all the jealous husbands, disappointed lovers, and psychotic male relatives o my female friends were to carry out one tenth of their threats against me, I should long ago have used up more lives than the traditional cat. No, it won't work, Betty."

"This is no bluff!" Betty cried. "I know Donald's temper, I tell you!"

"And out of deep concern for my life, you have come to warn me. Thank you. I am deeply touched. Thank you."

"You fool! Oh you fool!" Betty almost sobbed. "Isn't it plain enough? Can't you see who it is I'm worried about? Not you. Not even so much Dorothy! It's Donald! If he did anything that would put him in prison, I'd — I'd die!"

Bobby looked genuinely surprised.

"So it's like that with you and Don Hammond, is it? Having himself a little fling, eh? Then Ivy's suspicions — " He finished with an amused snort. "Very interesting, all this gossip. But hardly any of my concern. And I'm afraid I've done about all I can for Dorothy. I'll give her a call tomorrow, and if she can't come to terms then, I shouldn't be a bit surprised if the black-mailer got busy."

"You *can't* do that! You can't just ruin the lives of entire families because one girl won't play your sort of game! Think of the heartbreak, the misery it means, even if you refuse to believe that your own life may be endangered!"

"It's out of my hands," Bobby said. "Dorothy knows the conditions. If they can't be met, I'm sorry."

"My God, if you knew what you may bring down upon yourself! If you knew Don's temper as I do!"

Unimpressed, Bobby shrugged.

She had failed, then. The tragedy to which this was leading could not be put off, for Bobby Morgan was too complacent to believe and Dorothy was too distraught to reckon the consequences. She had failed Don at the one point in which she was really needed — to shield him from a part of his temperament which might be his destruction. Don, for whom she would have given her life, any part of herself...

Herself? The thought came spinning out of the alcoholic chaos which was her brain. Give herself? Was there something which she might barter with Bobby Morgan?

"Bobby..." Was that her voice? That exaggeratedly coy tone with its undercurrent of cunning? "Bobby, does it have to be Dorothy?"

"I don't understand," he puzzled.

"I mean — what if someone else could meet the terms? Wouldn't that do just as well? Couldn't . . " She paused to let her glance flutter meaningfully down over her body. "Couldn't *I* meet them?"

There seemed to be two of her. Two of Betty Brooks. One listening in frozen, horrified silence. The other saying,

"I could be nice — if I wanted to."

Bobby almost dropped his glass, but recovered his wits sufficiently to splash another finger of whiskey into it instead.

"Pardon me. I hardly expected such an offer."

"You'd like me," Betty purred. "After all, why Dorothy? She's not even grown yet. She's positively bony. *I'm* not."

"No," Bobby admitted, "you certainly aren't."

She was actually trying to sell herself, Betty realized. Tantalizing him, like a common street-walker.

"And if it's all been because you couldn't get her into bed — well, what about me?"

"A girl who dives off a boat and swims to shore half-naked, might be said to be hard to get," Bobby agreed.

Betty drew her skirt up a few revealing inches on her bare legs.

"I have nice legs, and nice — everything. You have a set of negatives I want. Fair trade?"

Bobby, seeming to suspect some trap, protested, "I didn't say I have those films."

"Of course not. But maybe the nice man might slip them through an open window while you're not looking."

"By George, he might at that!" Bobby leered. He made a move as though to drag her body to his, but Betty slipped away.

"Uh-uh," she chided. "Payment on delivery, and not before. And I can outrun you anytime, if I have to."

"You are, without a doubt, the damndest girl I ever met," Bobby chuckled.

Damned? Yes, she was damning herself, and she knew it in a vague way. But if she could go through with it, for Don ...

The radio was playing a slow blues with a jungle tom-tom beat. With the firelight behind her, Betty stood in the half light and rocked her hips.

"It's a deal," Bobby suddenly said, and with his words Betty felt a chill clutch at her heart like a hand. Bobby jumped up and continued, "I think I'll see if that man has been about, opening windows. When I come back, I think I should like to find you sitting on that bear-skin in front of the fireplace. Need I make a bad pun?"

"No," Betty said. "I know what's expected. You'll find what you want."

For a moment Bobby stood looking at her in a kind of puzzlement.

"Good God!" he said finally. "If ever a girl had me fooled, you did."

He tossed down his drink and left the room.

Alone, Betty clasped her face in both hands and fought off a sudden attack of trembling. What monstrous thing was she doing? In her heart she had often felt pity, but never understanding, as she passed some poor, bedraggled wretch of a drab in the streets. She could never believe that there were pressures which could drive women ot that resort. Yet here, on a different level, she was calculatingly entering her name on the roster of that sisterhood.

It was not too late! Now, while Bobby was gone, she could dash out to his car and leave. Or, even less drastically, she could tell him that she had changed her mind and demand to be driven home. She wasn't afraid of Bobby now, not the way she had been on his yacht. She had grown up since then. Yes, she could still save herself, and be done with a lover who lied and a giddy adolescent who whined when her folly caught up to her.

But the reflected image in the window was that of a somewhat unsteady girl tearing at her own clothing.

She pulled the dress over her head, dropped it in a heap on the couch, and paused for one last, jolting dose of raw whiskey.

She walked the length of the room to the fireplace. Her stockings were dry, or almost so. She knotted them nervously into a hard, tight ball and flung them in the direction of the couch.

The bearskin was warm and soft under her feet. She curled her toes into the hair, and experimentally poked her foot into the fanged, open jaws of the stuffed head. The glass eyes glared blindly as she settled herself on the glossy fur, her white body a strange contrast to the black hairiness. She looked down at her

bare thigh, the curve of her knee cradled in that unfamiliar softness. Then, overcome with shame for what she was doing, she
turned on her stomach and hid her face in the fur, running her
fingers through the deep pile in which her body lay half-buried.

What seemed like a step on the porch brought her head up
quickly. She listened, but did not hear it again. With the fire
crackling beside her and the radio only a few feet away, she
decided that it had been her imagination, her conscience working overtime, and she did not pay any attention when, later, she
heard a sound as though a car were driving off, for, just as that
happened, Bobby returned.

She sat up, curling herself into a concealing ball.

She stared at the fire while he moved close and stood over
her, his trouser-leg almost touching her shoulder.

"What a charming surprise package," she heard him say. "So
Kris Kringle has not forgotten me after all. And — oh yes. By
some remarkable coincidence, I happened to discover these on a
window-sill."

A glassine packet dropped beside her. Taking it up, Betty
spread out the negatives and tried to check the unpretty display
with the prints she had seen. Bobby, seeming to guess her purpose, said,

"They're all there."

One at a time Betty fed them to the flames. If only, she was
thinking, the inevitable memory of the next few hours could be
so easily destroyed!

Bobby moved restlessly as the pile of unburned film grew
smaller. Betty's lip curled.

"Don't worry," she said. "I won't try to welch. You'll get
everything you bought and paid for. I know what I am."

The gray light of dawn was slowly creeping through the bedroom. Betty was alone, and had been for some time, for Bobby,
satiated and sodden, had finally staggered to the living room for

yet another drink, and had not returned. She had not slept. Her mind was in too much of a turmoil.

She felt as though she had died a spiritual death, as though she had left behind her the world of things familiar to her and had entered an empty Limbo where she must wander in lonely loathing of herself for all time. Last year, last month, yesterday — all these were a million light years in the unretractable past, part of a different cosmos where there was love and affection and warmness between people. She had become something she hated, and nothing could ever make it right again.

And so she lay, sick with herself, and watched with dry, bitter eyes, the chill gray light come slowly creeping through the bedroom windows.

CHAPTER TWENTY-THREE

PLEASURE EXCURSION

"I beg your par— Oh, *hello* there! Don't tell me, now. It's . . Betty, isn't it? Betty Brooks. See? I never forget a face!"

"And everyone recognizes Janet Castle's," Betty replied. She was politely exaggerating, for her mind had puzzled quite blankly before the voice helped her remember the languorous, green-eyed woman who had once offered some trenchant advice from a deck chair on Bobby Morgan's yacht. "I wasn't racing you for a table, really I wasn't."

"Shouldn't have blamed you if you were," the actress replied, looking about the crowded little French restaurant. "This used to be a nice quiet place for luncheon, but it's getting almost too popular to bear."

A waiter hop-skipped up to them, holding up two fingers in a questioning gesture. A frown flickered across Betty's brow. She hadn't really wanted company for lunch, let alone anyone who reminded her of things she was trying to force out of her thoughts, but there seemed no way of saying so without being downright rude. And there was only one empty table in sight. Janet Castle looked to Betty before replying to the waiter, and Betty nodded.

"Martini?" Janet asked when they were seated.

"I don't think so. The onion soup will be fine to start with."

"I have a matinee today, so that means two martinis with lunch. I don't know why, but matinees always frighten me."

Betty murmured something, and as they gave their orders she noticed one or two heads turn in their direction. She should have been flattered, she supposed to find that the other woman had remembered her, and once, not too long ago, she would have felt quite important to be seen lunching with a Broadway celebrity. Now it wasn't that way at all. She had gone a long way in a few short months. It was hard to realize that it was only early fall, and that she could still count on the fingers of two hands the number of weeks that had passed since she had last lain long in Don's arms, certain that her happiness would last forever. So much had changed. So much had been lost.

"Are you living in Manhattan?" Janet was asking.

"No, I'm only in town for the day. Business connected with my father's estate. You know how chose things drag on."

Janet clucked sympathetically and spooned her *consomme aux berbes.*

"Sooner or later I suppose I'll move here," Betty said. "I don't know. Right now I have a temporary typing job in Westchester, just marking time."

In the polite way of people who do not know each other very well, they continued to make small talk throughout the halibut *à la provencale. As* the waiter came to take the dishes, however, Janet casually asked,

"Have you seen our friend Bobby Morgan lately? Since you took the plunge, so to speak?"

"I've seen him," Betty said grimly. Then she added, "I hate that man."

She hadn't meant to say it. It just slipped out, as though the emotion aroused by his name was too much to be contained. Janet Castle seemed unperturbed. She merely nodded and agreed,

"He's a very good man to hate."

Betty remained silent.

"It may be tactless of me to refer to what you did that night," the other woman finally continued, "but I'd like to say that I admired you for it. It was what I should have done once. Oh, not in a literal sense. But I shouldn't have let him frighten me as he did. I don't know whether I'd have been where I am today, but I'll bet I'd feel cleaner. On the other hand, he really had me over a barrel with trick pictures of his — or so I thought."

Betty's fork, carrying a bit of *souffle rhum,* stopped halfway to her mouth.

"Did you say … pictures?"

"Very indelicate pictures. Just imagine the lowest sort of French postcards and you have the idea. And I was in on the act. At least I thought I was. Some blackmailer was supposed to have taken them while I was too high on goof-balls and lush to know what I was doing. And Bobby, so the script ran, was the only person who could prevent them from being circulated."

Betty held her breath while the actress finished the last mouthful of her dessert and touched her lips with a napkin.

"And — what happened?" she ventured when she could bear the suspense no longer.

"I — well, I got the negatives of the prints. Later, when he'd had all the fun he wanted out of torturing me, Bobby twisted the knife by telling me the whole thing was a fake. He'd had some professional photographer do a clever paste-up and air-brush job, combining pornographic pictures with ordinary shots he'd taken of me from time to time. The negatives I had didn't mean a thing — just copies of the paste-ups, but it would have taken a photographer to detect it. Big joke on me. Ha-ha. I laughed and laughed."

She lighted a cigarette, then, glancing at the time, she exclaimed,

"Heavens, I've got to run! Sorry to break off this way, but it's later than I realized. Waiter!"

She tried to pay Betty's check, but Betty would not hear of it.

"Look me up when you're in town again," Janet Castle said. "I'm in the book. And thanks for the company."

"I should be thanking you," Betty replied. "More than you know."

Alone, she brooded over her *demitasse* for a long time, then ordered another So it had all been another of Bobby Morgan's sadistic jokes. No wonder Dorothy couldn't remember the incidents in those photographs — they had never occurred. The whole, miserable torture was based on a fraud, and she had done — that — for nothing. The grinning face of the man, sweaty with lechery, rose before her as it had been indelibly imprinted on her brain. It seemed to fill the whole room, the whole world. The entire world was made up of Bobby Morgan, grinning down at her, using her and laughing at the sport.

There was no one to whom she could turn, no one with whom to share this horrible secret so that this weight might rest less heavily on her shoulders. And what was her thanks for this? Dorothy's happiness? But that would have come anyway, after that brief time of fear which was, perhaps, only a just retribution for her foolhardy adventuring. For Bobby would never have sent those prints to Dorothy's or Oliver's family. Someone would surely have had enough faith in she girl to suspect some trick, to have had them carefully examined by a competent photographer. Vindictive though he might be, Bobby would not dare take such a chance, not with all trails leading to his door.

It was for Don, she had said, that she let herself be led into a degredation so foul that the mind turned from it, sickened. For Don. She felt a bubble of hysterical laughter forming in her throat.

Three nights previous she had seen Don on the street. He was alone, striding along in an angry way that made people instinctively give way as he passed. She had become aware of him when they were about a half a block apart, and she had stopped, not knowing what to do. And then he had seen her.

He had seen her and he had halted in his tracks as though he had encountered an invisible wall. Just for an instant they stood, staring across space at each other. Then Don had wheeled, almost knocking a passer-by into the gutter, and had crossed the street, heedless of traffic. He had turned the corner and disappeared.

For Don, who would not even recognize her in the street, this had been done? She felt the bubble well larger and larger in her throat, then burst. Her shoulders began to shake, and she knew that the odd, high-pitched sound which was filling the restaurant was her own laughter.

"Miss..." The large, black penguin beside her flapped his ridiculous wings and looked anxious. "Miss, are you all right?"

"Since when do penguins talk?" Betty asked. Then she saw that it was not a bird at all. The waiter was speaking to her.

"Is there something the matter, Miss? Is there something you need?"

"I'm all right, thank you. I was just having a bad dream."

The waiter looked at her strangely, genuinely concerned. Something like pity softened his quick eyes, and he said quietly,

"I am very sorry. It is not a good thing to have such bad dreams in the daytime."

"Do you know," Betty said, "I could almost believe that you mean that. It might just happen that you're the one human being in the whole, wide world who gives a damn."

The waiter looked for a moment as though his professional mask might slip.

"I am sorry," he repeated. And then, because his broken feet were aching and because he had long ago grown familiar with the ways of young women who were feeling alcoholically overwhelmed by the sadness of life, and because he had been trained as a waiter for many years, he went on,

"I am very sorry, but I must have this table now."

Betty walked through the busy streets of Manhattan as though through a dream. There was nothing in her bearing or manner which might have marked her apart from others, unless it were a somewhat deeper appearance of abstraction. She was, however, intensely aware of what was happening about her, as a traveler might have been in a strange land, and the apparent abstraction was only the evidence of her effort to translate things into a language she could understand.

For everything she encountered seemed to possess a deeper significance than she had ever realized. It was as though she were working some vast puzzle, in which even the least part had an important place. The chaos of colors, the cacophony of traffic sounds, the movements of people as individuals or *en masse,* all seemed to be part of a churning and only temporarily disarranged pattern. If only once she could find the key, everything would fall neatly into its proper niche, forming a complete and orderly whole.

The glimpsed headlines of newspapers, the mutterings of a drink-dazed derelict, the activity of some workmen who were tearing up a street — all these seemed to bear some subtle relationship to each other, the significance of which was slyly hidden from her. The dodging motion of a man who crossed her path as he hurried to a subway, and the quick, belly-slinking stealth of a cat leaving a cellar-way, the march of colored lights across an advertising sign, were all importantly connected, but she could not quite fit them together.

The TIMES building's gridle of lighted words flickered endlessly around the corner of the building to disappear into the oblivion of dead news. " … as hurricane moves northward. Winds ranging up to … "

A child ran out of a store, pointed a toy pistol at Betty, shouted "Bang!", and ran in again. A woman with a bit of paper in her hand studied street addresses, looked at the paper, and moved on, shaking her head.

"So I says to him," spoke a passing voice, loudly, "I says, for a lousy fifty bucks you expect me to do the whole thing by myself? What am I gonna get out of it? I says, you can take it and you can shove it. I don't care who it is, don't tell *me!* For a lousy fifty bucks I'm not breakin' my … "

A young man with lightly rouged cheeks moved delicately by, his plucked brows arched in a perpetual question to which he had long ago learned the answer.

What *was* it, that link which would tie all these together? There was a sense of looking through a badly focussed glass at an image whose outline could not quite be perceived. Or it was like trying to recall a forgotten poem, knowing that it would all come back to mind if one line, one word, even, could be grasped. There was something just out of reach, some bit of knowledge lodged in herself which could make it all clear. If she tried harder, just a little harder …

"Cucumber!"

That was the key! Everything was clear, now. Cucumber meant … meant … And then the sense of recognition faded. Faded like that false sense of memory which sometimes makes a strange street momentarily familiar, or makes some sequence of action appear a repetition of something dreamed. And fright came.

"I'm insane."

The words could not have been more clearly heard had she spoken them aloud.

She stepped into a doorway and, guided by some sly instinct to dissemble, to cover her actions by some pretense of normalcy, opened her purse and pretended to refresh her make-up. She remembered, now, an incident which had once taken place in a dentist's office. She had been given nitrous oxide, and, waking from its influence, she had been amusedly certain that she, and she alone, understood all the secrets of the universe — but they had been momentarily forgotten. The dentist had smiled at her excited efforts to convince him, and had explained that the hallucination was comon enough to have given the drug its name of laughing gas.

"If you *could* remember," he had told her, "I am afraid that the world would judge you to be quite insane."

But people who were insane never knew it — did they? Right at first, when it was beginning to come over them? If she was still able to realize that she was thinking nonsense, that proved that she was all right, didn't it?

I'm being hysterical, she told herself. Nothing else. I'll go home and try to get some rest, and tomorrow it will be all right. But I've got to get this whole rotten mess out of my mind. I've *got* to! And tomorrow, if I don't feel better, I'll see a doctor first thing. I've still got enough sense to do that.

She hailed a cab and asked to be driven to Penn Station.

The driver was in a talkative mood, and when a traffic light halted them for a few seconds, he leaned back and attempted a conversation.

"Guess that's some storm we got comin'," he offered.

"Really?" she asked. The last thing in which she was interested was the weather.

"Worsen last year, if it hits square," he said with a sort of pride, as though he had contrived it himself. "Glad I ain't on tonight."

At the station she bought a magazine, and throughout the journey back to Westchester she thumbed it constantly. But she was unable to concentrate, and the conversation of four men who were playing a perpetual bridge game kept intruding. Someone else had a portable radio and was constantly changing the station:

" — coastal waters from Block Island to Cape Hatteras. Small craft warnings have been displayed for several hours, and shipping activities have been suspended. On the basis of latest reports, present indications are that the storm movement may veer inland at a point approximately — "

"Good thing I got that garage door fixed last week," one of the bridge players observed as a dance band interrupted. "Last year my next door neighbor's red maple ended up on my front porch."

The trip seemed endlessly long. Yet there was nothing waiting at its end but a lonely furnished room and a solitary evening with her own thoughts. Perhaps she should go to a movie or — something. Anything to bring back to her the illusion of life. But she was suddenly too tired to think about it.

She half-dozed through the last miles of the trip. When she got off at her station the air was breathless and still. Before she reached her room, rain was quietly falling, but there was no movement in the air, no relief from the heavy, warning hush in the atmosphere. She put away the few purchases she had made and, still dressed, lay down upon the daybed. Within five minutes she was asleep.

CHAPTER TWENTY-FOUR
HELL'S DROP

IT was the wind which woke her, flinging the pouring rain against the windows in angry gusts, rattling the panes like an intelligent presence striving for entrance. She switched on a light and groped for the clock. It was after eight. She had slept like a person drugged.

She looked with distaste at the two-burner gas plate on which her cooking was done. She wasn't hungry, but she supposed she should eat. But first she would call Dorothy. It was only right that the girl should know what she had learned today. It wouldn't be necessary to explain how she had discovered the fraud, any more than it had been necessary to explain how she had secured the negatives. Dorothy had been too relieved to immediately ask questions when Betty had called that day to say they had been destroyed, and Betty had hung up in the middle of the girl's very real gratitude. She didn't really know why she should care enough to call Dorothy now, except that she remembered that she had liked her once, when she was capable of feeling. It would probably be a wonderful thing for Dorothy to learn that she had only been a fool, and not the thing that — that Betty Brooks had become.

The wall phone was down the hall, under a dim, bare bulb. Betty dialed the number and waited. The line was very noisy, and it was a long time before Dorothy herself answered.

"Yes?"

"This is Betty. I just called to tell you — "

"Oh, *Betty!*" Dorothy broke in. "It's a miracle that you called! I've been trying and trying to figure out a way to get in touch with you. Betty, something dreadful has happened! Don — Don found out!"

"Don *what*? How? How could he have? *What* did he find out? For God's sake, speak up!"

"It was an accident, Betty, truly. I didn't even know that picture was in my purse. It must have slipped out of the envelope I gave you. Anyway, Don was here tonight when I got in. He came to see Mother, I think, but she and Dad are both out of town — "

"Just tell me what happened, will you?"

'Well, I had my car keys in my hand, and when I went to put them in my purse I dropped it and everything spilled out. Don started to pick things up — and there was one of those pictures. Don turned white. Smithers was somewhere near, so Don took my arm and said, 'Let's go into the library.' He closed the door, and then he sat down and looked at me. He didn't say a word. Just looked at me."

Dorothy's voice faded, and Betty's first thought was that the connection had been broken. Trying to be calm, she said,

"Are you still there?'

"Betty, it was the most awful moment of my life. What was I to do? Then, when Don said, 'Do you carry these around for advertising purposes?', I couldn't stand it. I told him the whole thing — about the swimming party and not being able to remember, and about somebody trying to blackmail me through Bobby. When I tried to lie about Bobby wanting me to go to bed with him, I got all mixed up, and finally he knew all of it. Then he said, as though he were talking to himself, 'So that's why she did it!' He meant you, I think, but I didn't understand, and I said so. He said, 'You don't have to understand', and then he went to the cabinet where Daddy keeps a couple of revolvers, and he took out the biggest one and put it in his pocket. When he started for the door I got in front of him and tried to stop him, but he looked as though he didn't even know me any more. He just put his hand on my shoulder and gave me a shove that knocked me down, and he went out without even looking back."

"How long ago was this?" Betty put in quickly.

"Half, three-quarters of an hour ago. When the storm was just starting to get bad. Oh Betty, you can't know how I feel about this! I know he's gone looking for Bobby, and if he finds him before he calms down ... Betty, what can we do?"

Betty found that the fingers of her free hand, excitedly doodling on the cover of the phone book, were violently shaking. Watching them, she forced calmness to herself. When the tremor was only a slight trembling, she said,

"I don't know what you are going to do. I can't do anything."

"But Betty, perhaps the two of us, somehow — You know what will happen if they meet!"

"No," Betty said, "I won't even try. I've been kicked around enough, trying to help other people. It's driven me to a point where I'm actually ill, and I can't risk what might happen to me if it goes any further."

"Betty, Don is carrying a gun!"

"Policeman carry them too. Call the police, if you think it will help. Of course, in his present mood, Don might shoot anyone who tries to stop him, and even if he doesn't there'll be a terrific public scandal."

"That wouldn't help." Dorothy was crying now. 'If they arrested him, he'd simply brood about it, and sooner or later he'd try again."

"For God's sake!" Betty almost screamed. "I tell you I can't do anything! I can't! I've got to think of myself for once, no matter who else is hurt. Can't you see that? You can't know — you'll never know — what this has done to me already. But *I* know, and I tell you I'm through!"

"I'm sorry," Dorothy sobbed. 'I thought — Im sorry."

"If it will make you feel any better," Betty said, "I called to tell you to stop worrying about what you saw in those pictures. It never happened — not to you. Those things were just very clever fakes. I learned that today."

She slammed the receiver down on the hook and went back to her room. Water was being forced through the joints of the window frame, so she arranged a cloth to soak it up, and then stood looking into the black night. There was some lightning, but it was far off. Near-by was only the incessant downpour of rain and the steadily rising howl of the wind. She saw a sign hanging by one hinge, and a garbage can suddenly bounced across the street like a rolled toy.

Moving from the window, she turned on the radio. Both of the stations which usually carried classical music were presenting lectures, and the rest was a hodge-podge of come-and-get-me's, storm reports, and Mickey Mouse jazz. Snapping the set off, she lighted the gas and started coffee.

She had done the right thing. She knew there was a point at which one had to stop sacrificing for others, and she had reached and passed that point. Her experience of the afternoon had thoroughly frightened her, and her whole strength must now be directed toward herself, to guard against again moving so close to the abyss.

But she found herself watching the clock. Ten minutes, and she had coffee. That made twenty since she had called Dorothy. If Don had left the house three-quarters of an hour before that, he would have time to — She mustn't think of that.

Ten minutes more to drink her coffee and try to read the magazine bought in Penn Station. Another cup? Another five minutes. A loud crash somewhere outside made her jump as a plate glass window collapsed before the wind. She watched the second hand of the clock moving with electric smoothness around and around its implacable face.

What had Don said to Dorothy? "So that's why she did it." What did that mean? Dorothy still believed that those films had been obtained by some unknown, but perfectly innocent means. Don, who had seen her drive off with Bobby, might have suspected something more, but —

She jumped up and thumbed through an address book. There was one thing she could do which would not involve her too deeply, and yet might avert tragedy. She could call Bobby Morgan and simply tell him to disappear, tell him that Don was out to kill him. Bobby might get out of sight or he might call the police for protection. He would never, she was sure, stand up to Bon alone.

Back in the dim hallway, she called all the numbers Dorothy had given her, one after the other. At each she got the same negative reply when she asked if Bobby was there. But at one place, a nightclub, she was told,

"Funny thing — a fellow was just in here looking for him, but I couldn't help him either."

Don really was searching for Bobby, then. Searching hard, and he evidently had a good idea of where to look.

There was only one number left — that of the cabin at Hell's Drop. It was an out of town call, of course, and she had to ring the operator.

"I don't know if I can get you through," the girl said. "We've been having trouble with the lines out that way."

Eventually she could hear a faint voice respond on the other end of the wire. The local operator. She could hear the two of them talking, the second one a thin wave which finally said,

"I'm afraid I can't connect you. Several poles are already down, here. I believe that line is knocked out."

"Please try," Betty broke in. "It's terribly important. *Terribly.*"

The line crackled.

"Sorry," the wavering voice insisted. "I can't — One moment, pleeuzh. I think..."

She heard the faint, familiar sound of a phone being rung. Then, as though from another planet, Bobby Morgan said,

"Hello?"

"This is Betty Brooks. I have something I —"

"Hello?"

"Hello — can you hear me?"

"Is someone there? Hello? Hello?"

And then silence.

"Operator — "

"I am sorry. I cannot get through to your party. That circuit is now completely dead."

In her room again, Betty paced the floor, chewing the knuckles of one hand. If Don decided to go to Bobby's cabin, if the two met face to face in that isolated spot, nothing could save Bobby. It would mean murder, and she would have on her conscience the knowledge that she had not done all she could to prevent it.

The clock drew her eyes again. In the time she had wasted since calling Dorothy, she could have been well on the way to Hell's Drop. Instead, she had stayed here arguing with herself while precious minutes — those minutes which might mean all the difference — slipped away.

For the third time that night she went to the phone. But this time she was running.

Dorothy answered on the second ring.

"Can you drive in this storm?" Betty demanded without preliminary.

"Oh — Betty. I thought —"

"Can you?"

"Yes."

"Well, you're driving to Hell's Drop, if we can get through. Don't take the Jaguar. We want more than canvas over our heads."

"The station wagon?"

"All right. Here's my address. Its close enough so that you should be here in a matter of minutes."

"I'm halfway out the door now," Dorothy said.

Safely indoors, Betty had not realized the full intensity of the storm. Now, as Dorothy skidded around a corner, she could feel the wind lift the car like a giant hand and nudge it dangerously near the curb. Peering through the windshield, she could see only a few feet ahead, and she knew that Dorothy was far overdriving the limit of safety. There were few cars on the streets, however, and no pedestrians. The greatest danger was that of coming suddenly upon some mass of wind-torn rubble.

All about them were evidences of the storm, which had not even yet reached its height. Gaping store windows were on every block, billboards were crumpled like cards, hotel canopies were twisted masses of collapsed framework and torn canvas. Huge signs had crashed in heaps of broken glass and crushed metal, and the sidewalk before one building was littered with the remains of an entire cornice. An occasional lone policeman worked with bits of rope to block off an area beneath a sagging marquee, or stood guard before a shop open to loot.

Block by laggard block they worked their way to the highway — and even here the pace was maddeningly slow. Careening from one side of the road to the other when the wind struck broadside, the car moved forward in uneven starts as it bored through the gusts.

"Ignition's getting wet," Dorothy said once. "Feel the engine skip? Just pray it doesn't conk out."

But for the most part she drove in silence, eyes narrowed with the strain, her mouth pressed tightly into a thin, straight line. A quarter of an hour dragged by. A half. A full hour.

Suddenly a dark mass loomed on the roadway before them. Dorothy wrenched at the wheel, and her foot struck the brake. The station wagon lurched into a sickening skid, moving broadside toward the uprooted elm which lay almost across the highway. Then the motor raced as she jabbed the accelerator and twisted the wheel back. Tires spun, caught, and the car straightened out for an instant. So closely that Betty heard one fender scrape the tree, they slithered by and went into another, briefer skid. Then the car rolled to a stop.

"Close," Betty said.

'Too damned close. And I stalled the engine."

The starter ground, but the engine did not catch.

"I was afraid of that," said Dorothy.

She tried again, with no result. The palms of Betty's hands began to grow moist. Once more the starter churned and failed. Dorothy hooked a cigaret on her lip and took two heavy drags.

'Do you suppose we could push this thing to that grade up ahead? If we can get it rolling..."

"But why? The starter turns all right."

"I don't know why. Don told me once. It works — sometimes."

They climbed out of the car and, one on each side, strained to move it. An inch, at first. Then two. Six. Then it was moving more freely. Moved freely for a few feet, then slowed to a stop.

"We can't — can't do it all at once," Dorothy panted.

"I'm not sure we can do it at all," Betty said grimly.

"We've got to."

The slope was perhaps half a city block away. It took them twenty minutes to reach it. Then they were back in the car, and it was gathering speed on the free roll downgrade.

With the car in second, Dorothy let out the clutch. The engine sputtered. Coughed. And died.

"It's *got* to work," Betty whispered. "It's *got* to."

Then, miraculously, the engine was running. Erratically, at first — but running.

The dirt road, as they turned onto it, looked worse than Betty had imagined. They drew to a stop, and with sinking heart she thought of the narrow, twisting miles ahead. Branches and saplings were scattered here and there in a sea of mud. Rocks had washed down from the hillside and lay partially buried in the muck.

"What do you think?" Dorothy asked.

"We'll go as far as we can," Betty said. "Then we'll walk."

Lightning began to flash about them, and Betty sensed that the storm was slowly nearing its peak. The roar of the blasting wind was so great that, even in the car, it was necessary to shout. Twigs and small branches, long denuded of leaves, fell almost constantly, and more than once Betty winced as one greater than the rest crashed on the car top with a roar that almost split her eardrums.

During the next few crawling miles, the car was seldom out of its lowest gear. Time after time they stopped until some obstacle could be moved out of the way. At one point they passed beneath a power pole toppled across the road with its splintered top leaning into the top of a tree, broken wires sparking in impotent, rasping anger as they brushed together a foot or two over the top of the car.

As they moved into the last third of those endless miles, Dorothy said,

"Betty, have you noticed anything unusual about the road?"

"This is no time to be funny," Betty snapped.

'I wasn't trying to be. I meant — there, see that big branch, the way it's crushed down? A car has driven over that — And I'm sure that log has been rolled aside. Haven't you seen that the further we go, the fewer things are blocking our way? Somebody is ahead of us, and we're catching up because he has to stop more often. It *must* be Don. Nobody else would be in here tonight."

Betty nodded and hunched in her seat. Now that the moment was near when she must again face Donald, she began to dread it. What could she say to him, what words could she use to make him understand and keep him from exacting a fearful vengeance from Bobby? What Bobby Morgan had done could never be defended. Her only only hope was to make Don see that he would only bring more tragedy to all of them, the innocent along with the guilty, if he gave full vent to the rage which was in him.

If only it was not already too late! If they could overtake him now, before he reached the cabin, perhaps...

"Hurry!" She exclaimed.

"I'm doing the best I can," the girl protested.

A boulder the size of a bushel basket bounded down a slope and across the road ahead of them, missing the front wheels by inches.

"I'm doing the best I can," Dorothy repeated.

As they maneuvered around a hair-pin turn, Betty suddenly saw the flash of car lights ahead. They disappeared, then were in sight again. Then they were not moving at all.

"Something has stopped him," Betty said. "We'll be up to him in a minute."

The words were hardly out of her mouth when the car struck a patch of leaves. Slowly the back end of the station wagon slid to the right, while Dorothy fought the wheel. Then, with a jolt, they slipped into the ditch. They got out to inspect the car.

The car was undamaged, but it took time for Dorothy to manage to rock it back onto the road — precious minutes of time, during which the lights of the car ahead moved on and disappeared. When they caught up again, the other car was swinging into Bobby's driveway.

Dorothy killed the engine and yanked the car to a slithering stop. Don was already crossing the clearing in front of the sprawling cabin. He turned and looked in the direction of the station wagon, but he did not stop. Betty jumped from the car.

"Don!" she cried into the deafening gale. "Don, it's Betty! Wait!"

He saw her, and he paused. Then he went on. Leaning into the wind, he stamped up onto the porch and tried the latch. It seemed to be locked. He hammered the door once. Then, as Betty fought her staggering way through the flooding downpour, he set his foot against the door and kicked against it twice. The second time it burst open, and he stalked in, with Dorothy and Betty a few seconds behind him.

Bobby Morgan, with the usual glass in his hand, was roughing it in a boyish slack-suit and a dressing gown patterned with leaping sword fish. On the couch, roughing it in a filmy negligee, was Ivy Dorset.

CHAPTER TWENTY-FIVE

BREACH OF PROMISE

BOBBY Morgan was the first to speak.

"Will someone please shut that door?" he said with an exaggerated air of politeness. "We're using oil lamps because of the failure, and I'm afraid they're not hurricane-proof."

Dorothy put all her weight against the door and managed to press it shut. The curtains, which had billowed like sails, slowly settled back in place, and Bobby casually righted a bridge lamp which had toppled. Ivy had not moved, and Don was staring at her, his face drained of expression.

"As you can see," Bobby Morgan said, tipping his glass, "we were hardly expecting guests on such a night. Certainly not in such numbers, or so — unannounced. You will pardon me if my hospitality seems somewhat strained."

"Damn it!" Ivy exclaimed, "Give me something to put on. I'm not giving an exhibition."

Looking somewhat annoyed, Bobby gave up his dressing gown, and she quickly slipped into it.

"Don," Betty said. "Don, listen. I have to talk to you."

He appeared not to have heard. He was still staring at Ivy.

"Strange," he said. "I didn't expect this. I don't know why. I must have been blind."

"Now look, old boy," Bobby said, "I know this must be rather upsetting and all that, but if you look at things from a realistic point of view, it's not necessary at all, you know. I mean, things aren't quite what they appear to be on the surface, you understand, and we've got to be a little bit tolerant once in a while if we're going to get along. After all, we *are* civilized human beings, aren't we?"

"Stop staring at me like that!" Ivy suddenly shouted at Donald. "You came here spying on me, and you found what you were looking for! There's no need for you to act as though it were all a big surprise!"

"Donald ... "

"And *you!*" Ivy turned on Betty. "You put him up to this! You brought him here, didn't you? I knew you were a dirty little sneaking guttersnipe the first time I saw you! Thought you saw a chance to marry into some money, didn't you? Working for the Hammond family, were you? How — on your back?"

"Don't you dare, you — you witch Jezebel!" Dorothy came to Betty's defense. "Don't dare talk about Betty like that!"

She drew her hand back and was about to slap Ivy across the face when Betty intervened and caught her wrist.

"Don't bother, Dot," Betty said tiredly. "None of us are here with clean hands."

"Exactly," Bobby Morgan chimed in. "After all, these things are part of life, eh Donald? I mean, well, while Ivy was in Euorpe, you weren't exactly a celibate yourself, you know."

"You're damn right he wasn't," Ivy exploded. "And after I found his concubine planted cosily where he could have her any time he reached out his hand, it took a detective about twenty-four hours to report to me that they'd spent a week together in the woods. And as for his precious little sister here, who pretends to be so innocent and then goes running off to swimming parties where nobody brings a swimming suit, maybe she'd like to show her brother what I saw a few weeks ago! Bobby, where are those pictures you showed me? Not just the ones on the beach, the others?"

"Shut up, Ivy," Donald growled.

"Yes, Ivy," Bobby said uneasily. "No need to bring up things like that, really. Now if we all just act like reasonable, civilized people, talk this over — "

"Donald!" Dorothy broke in, "you mustn't believe those pictures! They're fakes! Ask Betty!"

Don looked at Betty.

"Is that true?" he asked.

"It's true," she said. "But Don, please don't... don't do anything that we'll all be sorry for. Take Dorothy home, Don. It will be the best thing you can do for all of us, believe me."

"A capital idea!" Bobby said heartily. "No use going off half-cocked, old man. Get a good night's rest, think things through, and tomorrow the whole thing may look different. No use acting like a group of savages. We're all adults, with some idea of what goes on in the adult world. You had your little fling while Ivy was in Europe, so it's not logical for you to be so upset over tonight, is it now? Sauce for the goose, and all that, you know."

"Bobby, you're drunk and you're talking too much," Ivy snapped.

"Am I? Well, perhaps, since I've been having drink for drink with you. But I don't like the notion of taking the full brunt of the blame for this, just because you happened to be caught with me instead of someone else. Why don't you speak up? If you and Donald have something to settle between you, I'm sure it can be done without involving me, particularly."

He turned to Donald.

"You understand what I mean, of course. To put it quite plainly, I could name half a dozen others with whom Ivy maintains a sort of perpetual affair. God knows how many that last only for a night or two — but Ivy will probably tell you if you use the proper methods of interrogation. She is — er — quite susceptible to certain forms of persuasion. So you see, there's not much point in getting all steamed up about me."

Ivy let go with a stream of invective which would have done justice to a dock-walloper.

"You yellow-bellid snake!" she finally ended up. "You don't give a damn for anyone else when your own hide is threatened, do you? Well, crawl, and spill your guts! I'm through with both of you, and I hope you all burn in hell! You, Don Hammond! You've been trying to find some excuse to break off our engagement ever since I came home. Well, now you've got it — so what? You heard what he said, and it's so. Going to marry your school-day sweetheart, like they do in the movies, were you? Only one thing was wrong — the little girl had grown up and had ideas of her own. There was just one thing you had that she needed. Money. Lots and lots of pretty money. So she stuck like a burr after she maneuvered you into proposing. Tonight changed all that, so I can tell you what I really think of you. I think you stink, and the only part of you I really want is a check, if my lawyers can get anything out of you on a breach of promise suit."

"That seems to cover the situation pretty well," Donald said. His voice sounded suddenly loud, for with an abruptness that was startling, the wind outside had died. The dead center of the storm was passing, and the air was heavy and still. With a contemptuous snort, Ivy, disregarding her audience, put aside Bobby's dressing gown and began to put on her clothes.

"However," Donald continued, swinging back to Bobby Morgan, "that isn't what I'm here for. I came to take care of this rat."

Bobby took a nervous step or two backward as Don moved toward him.

"I told you once that I'd kill you if you didn't leave Dorothy alone," Don said, his voice scratching like a file on sheet metal. "I'm not sure that I meant it then, but after what you've done to her since that time, I know I mean it now. I set out tonight to kill you, Morgan. I'm going to do it. With my bare hands, if I can do it, and if I can't do that..."

"No need for anything quite so drastic, old boy," Bobby said placatingly. "No harm has come to the girl, you know. Maybe it wasn't the best joke in the world, making up those pictures, but I didn't expect her to take it so seriously. Try to calm down a bit, can't you?"

"Calm down? I've had plenty of time to calm down. And all the time I was searching gin mills for you, and all the time I was driving out here, I was becoming more and more sure that there's only one thing to do about you. And I'm going to do it."

Bobby turned quickly to Dorothy.

"Say something!" he almost screeched. "Tell him the truth — that nothing ever happened to you while you were with me! Nothing ever happened to you here! You had too much to drink one night and fell asleep, that's all."

"Don, it's true," Dorothy said. "I never let him touch me. He had me worried sick, but nothing ever happened, really."

"Didn't it?" Don asked. His eyes turned to Betty with a meaning that was deeper than the words. And suddenly Betty understood. The step she had heard on the porch that night, the car driving away — they had not been imaginary. That explained Don's words to Dorothy: "So that's why she did it." And that explained why he had refused to recognize her on the street, later. Knowing that she was with Bobby Morgan that night, he had left Ivy and come to the cabin looking for her, And, stepping onto the porch to ring the bell, he had seen her lying naked before the fire, waiting for Bobby.

Two bright spots of color appeared on her cheeks, and she looked away from Don's steady gaze.

"Really, now," Bobby whined, "this is the Twentieth century. One doesn't go about threatening violence over a bit of fun."

"Fun? So that's your idea of fun, is it?" Don demanded. His voice rose as the wind outside began to howl again. "Well, this — is — my — idea — of — fun!"

He had sprung forward and grasped Bobby's shirt-front in one fist, yanking him to tiptoe. Punctuating each word with a violent wrench, he shook the other man like a limp rag, then with a single heave flung him backward against a chair, which collapsed as Bobby crashed into it.

"Stop it!" Dorothy screamed, rushing forward. "Donald, please, you don't know what you're doing!"

Donald brushed her off as he might have pushed aside a playful puppy.

"I know what I'm doing," he snarled. "Just leave me alone with him! Get out of the room, all of you!"

"Don't you do it!" Bobby cried in a high-pitched voice. "Call the police! He's insane, I tell you!"

"Just mad," Donald said. "Mad clean through."

Betty shot a glance at Ivy, who had stepped forward, fastening her dress. Ivy's eyes were shining, and an expression which was both eager and hungry was upon her face. With a shock of disgust, Betty realized that the other woman was actually enjoying the scene.

Donald lunged and grappled with Bobby just as he tried to dart past to the doorway. Bobby struck out, catching Don full on the mouth, but before he could follow up that momentary advantage, a short, chopping blow had knocked him to his knees.

"Why don't you stop him?" Bobby screamed from the floor. "Ivy, do something! Hit him with something!"

"Go to hell, you yellow punk!" Ivy said. "I hope he kills you!"

Betty lifted the phone from its cradle. It was dead, as she knew it would be. She dropped it back.

And now Bobby began to fight back. He fought desperately. Thrust backward over an overturned table, he scrambled around it on hands and knees and tried to tackle Don's legs. Seconds later, as he lurched near the fireplace, he seized a heavy poker and tried to crush it down on Don's skull, only to have it torn from his grasp and flung with a crash through a window. Kneeling, gouging, clawing, he had only one objective — to get to the door and escape somewhere into the night. Once, as Don fell headlong over a kicked-up rug, his hand was on the very latch, but before he could pull it open he was knocked staggering and spinning along the wall, pulling down a large section of draping as he tried to keep his feet.

The room was fast becoming a shambled wreck. Bobby's bloodshot eyes were bulging like those of a man choked, and his breath was a rasping gasp as he gagged on the blood he had swallowed. Betty felt faint and dizzy as she looked at the curious tableau which the other two women made — the one frozen in impotent, speechless horror, the second craning her neck anxiously, so as not to miss any part of the brutal scene. She could sense coming over her again that feeling of facing a puzzle which she must solve.

And suddenly she screamed.

It began with a low moaning sound in her throat, and then it began to build, louder and louder, rising in pitch at the same time, welling out of the seething sea of emotion within her, until all the protest and rejection of the wrongness of things was contained in its knife-like, raging tone.

Don, his fist drawn back to drive into Bobby's face, paused and turned, and Bobby stumbled away.

"I can't stand any more of this!" Betty cried. "*I — just — can't stand — any — more!*"

She ran to Don, and, facing him, took his right arm in both her hands.

"Listen to me," she demanded. "Listen hard, and try to understand every word. I'm not going to let you do anything more to me, do you hear? I've been through the humiliation of learning that you had a fiancée, that I was nothing more than the — the concubine Ivy called me. I've had my heart break when I learned you weren't what I thought. But I've had more than that, because I couldn't stop loving you. I got mixed up with Bobby Morgan only to prevent you from doing what you're trying to do now. You saw me here on the night that it happened, so you know how those fake pictures were bought back — and all to keep you from finding out about them, because I still loved you and couldn't bear to think of you doing yourself an irreparable injury. Yes, I prostituted myself, because I thought that prostitution was a lesser crime than murder.

"And for what? To find that you wouldn't speak to me on the street, to find that Bobby's threats had been wholly empty, to be so beaten down by shame and remorse and heartbreak that I'm on the point of breaking up mentally. And now you are deliberately trying to beat a man to death anyway. Do you think I can stand that? *Do you think my mind can take the knowledge that everything I've done has been for nothing at all?"*

"Don, look out!" Dorothy suddenly cried.

Bobby Morgan was weaving around a table, a large and smoking oil lamp tiltingly held in one drawn-back fist.

"Get out of my way," he said. "If you make one move to stop me, I'll throw this in your face."

He took a slow step forward. With one motion Don shoved Betty aside and scooped into his pocket. His hand came out holding an ugly-nosed, heavy revolver. For the tick of three seconds, neither man moved.

"Go ahead. Shoot." It was Betty's voice, drenched with bitterness. "Murder him, and someday when my child asks about his father, I can say he died bravely in the electric chair. I'm sure he'll consider you quite the hero."

Don's jaw dropped in astonishment as the words filtered through the tension and the hot, red rage. He turned away from Bobby, and the gun barrel wavered.

"Child?" he said. "You mean I — you .. ?"

Betty looked steadily at him.

"Will you come home with Dorothy and me now?" she asked.

At that instant Bobby flung the lamp.

Don ducked, and it bounded off his shoulder, its chimney shattering. Then, full on Ivy's chest it struck, knocking her backward into a tangle of torn curtains. An oily puffball of black smoke snaked out of the smouldering lamp, then flickered and was flame. Droplets of liquid fire dripped from Ivy's arms as she flung them across her face. Aflame from her waist upward, she fought the door open and, with a piercing scream, dashed into the wind-torn night, a living torch. For a horrible second, everyone was too hypnotized to move. Then they went after her.

CHAPTER TWENTY-SIX

CHIPPIE

THEY caught her at the edge of the woods. Don flung himself on her and rolled her on the ground, smothering the flames with his coat and his own body. She sat on her haunches then, rocking back and forth, her only sound a continuous soft mewing.

"A doctor," Dorothy said. "We've got to get her to a doctor."

Betty crouched near the dark, huddled figure.

"See if the station wagon will start," she said to Dorothy. "Ivy, can you walk? We have to get you to one of the cars."

She had to bend low to hear the answer.

"I can walk," Ivy said. "There's nothing wrong with me. But my hair got burned off, didn't it? And it takes so long to grow."

The words bubbled out from a hole that had once been lips.

They got her to her feet and walked her down to the driveway. The flames from inside the house were beginning to lick through the windows by then, and in the glare Ivy's face could now be seen.

"Oh God," Dorothy whispered. She ran ahead to start the car.

Ivy was placed on a seat in the back of the station wagon, with Betty next to her. Dorothy, behind the wheel moved over to let Don drive.

"Where's Bobby?" Betty said. "We'll need all the help we can get to clear the road."

'Hell!" Don exploded. "I forgot about him. I slugged him just after he threw that lamp. I didn't see him get up again. Maybe he's still in there."

He jumped out of the car and ran toward the house. Betty took one look at the holocaust it had become and cried after him,

"You can't go in there! Not the way it is now!" She grabbed Dorothy's shoulder. "Stay with Ivy," she said, and then she was racing toward the burning house after him. For an instant she saw his form silhouetted in the doorway, and then it was gone. She began to pray aloud.

A blast of heat almost threw her back as she reached the porch. But Don — Don was somewhere in there. She threw one arm across her face and dove into the inferno, shouting his name.

Inside, it was worse than she could have believed — and neither Bobby nor Don were to be seen. She ran across the room and flung open a blistering door which led to a bedroom. Nothing. Another door. But that was only a closet.

"Don! Don!" she begged. "Oh Don, my love, where are you?"

And then, like a man walking the corridors of hell, Don appeared through the smoke which rolled through the hallway.

"Out," he choked. "He's not in here."

He clasped her shoulder, and they fled just as one wall sagged inward and collapsed behind them.

Dorothy was running up the path.

"Damn it!" Betty berated her as she came up to them, "I told you to stay with Ivy! You know she shouldn't be left alone like that!"

"Ivy — Ivy — " Dorothy swayed, and Betty clutched her by both shoulders, shaking her fiercely.

"What about Ivy?" she demanded. What's happened?"

"Ivy — she — oh, it's awful! This whole night has become a horrible nightmare! She ran ... "

"You've got to stop this! What are you trying to say?"

"After — after you left, I sat there in the car with Ivy, watching you both go into the house. I didn't notice when she reached up and moved the rear-view mirror so she could see herself in it. The first thing I knew was when she moaned, and when I turned, there she was, looking at what was left — looking at her face. Her eyes — you know how they were. Then she looked at me. I'll never forget that moment until I die!"

"*What happened*?" Don insisted.

"She — she got out the rear door before I could stop her. I shouted to you, but you couldn't hear me, of course. And I was out of the car almost as soon as she was. I couldn't catch her. She ran toward the Drop. She ran, and she kept on running. And when she reached the edge she didn't stop and she didn't even pause. She didn't jump. She *ran* over. She ran. She . . "

"Show us where. Exactly where." Don hurried Dorothy along ahead of him.

They stood at the spot which Dorothy indicated. In front of them the cliff dropped sheerly to a mass of broken, sea-lashed boulders. Unseen, the pounding breakers could be heard thudding below.

"Not a chance," Donald said. "At least it was quick."

"I don't know what to say to you," Betty told him. "You reach a point, finally, where there just aren't any words left."

"You don't have to say anything. I loved her when we were kids, and I thought I loved her up until several months ago, some time before I met you. Now it's as though a stranger had died. It may sound harsh to say this, but Ivy did the only thing she could have done. She couldn't have lived like — like what she would have been. She didn't have enough self inside."

"Look!" Dorothy said suddenly. "There's something out there on the water! No, this way, a little way out from the boat house."

"It's a boat! A little cabin cruiser, isn't it?" Betty said. "You don't suppose Bobby . . . "

A long, flickering flash of lightning served to answer. In its extended glare, the perpetually boyish figure of Bobby Morgan could be seen as he stood at the wheel. Outlined as they were with the blazing cabin behind them, Bobby must have seen them too, for, with a regal gesture of contempt, he turned and cheerfully thumbed his nose.

"The fool!" Don exclaimed. "What's he trying to do? He's been around water enough to know he can't possibly keep that boat afloat once he's past the lee of the Drop."

They stood, the three of them, on the edge of Hell's Drop until their straining eyes could no longer find the outlines of the boat.

As they turned away and started back to the cars, the roof of the cabin fell in, and a mighty shower of sparks ascended like an offering to some powerful and obscene god of violence.

Next day, at a point some miles distant, the sea gave back what had once been Ivy Dorset. The body of Bobby Morgan was never found, though bits of wreckage from his boat were occasionally discovered.

CHAPTER TWENTY-SEVEN

SACCHARINE SONG

"I'M real sorry you're leaving, Miss Brooks. When I get tenants I like, I hate to see them leave."

"I'm sure you'll have someone in here very soon, Mrs. Jones."

"Oh, I won't have any trouble renting the room. It's just that you never know what kind you're going to get when you start taking in guests. Why, do you know, I've had girls come in here — nice looking girls, mind you — and the first thing I knew there was men coming and going at all hours, and I don't know what all. That's why when I get somebody nice and quiet like you I try to do all I can to make them comfortable. I run a decent, respectable house, and I always say —"

A heavy knock at the door interrupted.

"Come in," Betty called.

Don walked through the doorway. Mrs. Jones frowned. Of course if he was a relative, or something like that...

"I thought I asked you not to come here," Betty said. She snapped a suitcase shut.

"So you did, but when Dorothy told me that you were leaving town I felt it was time to see you. After all, as the father-to-be of your unborn child — "

Mrs. Jones gave a little shriek. Snatching up the keys which she had come to get, she marched indignantly out of the door, being careful to leave it open.

"What's the matter with her?" Donald asked. "Doesn't she like children?"

"You know very well that I'm not going to have a baby," Betty said. "I told you that before. When I saw you with that gun in your hand, I had to say something to keep you from using it, that's all."

"Yes, I know, but I rather like the idea. I *like* thinking of myself as a father-to-be."

Betty continued to pack. Don sat down on the bed beside the open bag.

"You haven't given me a chance to really talk to you since that night at Hell's Drop. There are some things I think you ought to know about some of my actions, and I believe I have a right to get them said."

"Go right ahead. Just remember I'm catching a train."

"First of all, I want you to know that I was trying to break up with Ivy before I ever met you, even before she sailed for Europe. That's point number one."

"All right."

"Point number two: I knew she was going to be hard to handle, and that if she heard about you she'd raise an awful row, probably drag your name through the courts, and mess things up generally. That's why, when she got back, I gave her time which I shouldn't have taken from that project we were working on at the lab — to try to argue her into agreeing to call the whole thing off. I had an idea that she was playing around, but I didn't know with whom, and I don't like the notion of sending detectives out to snoop."

"You could have told me about her."

"That was my big mistake, and I admit it. All I can say is that I was terribly afraid of losing you, and you're the sort of girl who would fade out of the picture if she thought someone else had a prior claim on something she wanted."

"Maybe I was once. Not any more. From now on, it's me first. I'm looking out for myself from here on in."

"I don't believe that, you know. Anyway, after you disappeared, I continued to try to break off with her, but by that time she had decided that she was going to stick around, hell or high water. I was just ready to tell her that I was through, and she could take me to court or do anything else she cared to, when I saw you and Morgan on the street that night."

He held up a pair of very sheer panties and looked through them at the light. Betty took them from him and dropped them in the bag.

"I had to see you. I had to explain some of the mess. So, as soon as I could, I got rid of her and went looking for you and Bobby. Someone told me he was spending a lot of time at his cabin, so I drove out there. When I happened to glance in that window — well, I didn't know what had been going on between you and Dorothy. Can you understand how I felt?"

"Yes, I think I can. I don't blame you for that. I don't blame anyone but myself for anything that's happened to me, but I'm going away from the place where it happened. I have my father's affairs pretty well straightened out now, and by a stroke of luck I discovered that I have an interest in some patent rights that will give me a little money. So I'm going to find a little town out west somewhere where they never heard of me, and I'm going to teach school for the rest of my life. And I'm going to mind my own business and I'm going to be very happy."

"I've been thinking of going off on a little trip of my own," Don said. "Up to my camp. You ought to see it up there at this time of year. The leaves are just turning about now, and at night the stars seem closer than at any other time of the year. You know that trail up to Bald Mountain?"

"The east trail?" Betty frowned. She was standing with a toothbrush in her hand and seemed to have forgotten what she was going to do with it.

"No, the west trail, starting at that big rock you called — what did you call it?"

"The Hen with Chickens."

"That's the one. Well, if you go up there about a mile and branch off to the left you come to a place where you can look down over that whole valley, and you never saw anything like it in your life. Then, back on the other side of the Sweet Branch, there's a pond I always meant to take you to, but it's best right now. For just two weeks during the year the sun slants across the mountains in such a way that when it's going down you'd swear the whole thing was pure gold. Bass in there . ." He held his hands several inches apart and cocked his head critically. " .. that long."

"Liar!" Betty laughed. "You almost believe that yourself, don't you?"

"Well, they *must* be in there — I never caught any. And sometimes about this time of year there's a freak run of trout, and if you go up by that spot where I threw that little bridge across the creek, sometimes you can find old Grumpy trying to fish them out with his paw. And those little deer we saw early in the year — by now they — "

"Stop it, will you?" Betty exclaimed, flinging the toothbrush down. "You know how I feel about that place."

"Yes, it's lovely. But it's going to be pretty lonely up there alone at night, darning my own socks, talking to myself... "

He reached into a pocket and took out a bit of golden fluff.

"Here's your Golden Nymph, if you want it," he said. "I've been carrying it around with me every since we came back. But... "

Betty was crying. He stood up then and put his arms around her.

"Couldn't we put those bags in my car instead of on a train? And couldn't we sort of stop by at the license bureau and get started on being married?"

Betty clung to him and reached for his lips.

"Oh, Don," she said. "We could, we could."

Half an hour later as they were driving away from the place, a cab shot suddenly from the curb. Don stood on the brake and stopped with an inch to spare. Then he said something under his breath. The cab driver said something which was more audible. Don opened the car door and had started to get out when Betty laid a wifely hand on his arm.

"Temper, dear," she reminded.

Don slumped back and muttered. He sat up and looked at the cab driver. He tipped his hat.

"Sorry," he said. "All my fault."

He tipped his hat again and drove on, leaving behind him the most astounded man on the Eastern seaboard. And that very day the cab driver helped an old boy scout across the street. And when pay-day came, instead of going to the tavern as usual, he bought a television set of his own and soon fell into the habit of spending his evenings at home in the bosom of his family, so he lived happily ever after also.